When I heard Ms. Hart's response, it was all I could do to keep from gasping.

"You can't be serious."

"Why not?" Mr. Homer demanded. "You told me yourself Carla did a fine job at the audition. You just said you expected her to steal the show."

"Yes . . . in a *character* part. But let's face it. For all her acting talent, Carla Farrell does not exactly *look* the part of a star."

There it was. She said it straight out. And even though I knew in my heart that she was right, hearing someone say it didn't do much to make me feel any better.

I never heard the end of the conversation. Instead, I took off. All I wanted was to get home, to my own house, to my own room, where I could close the door and shut out the entire world.

Finally, it was getting to be time for that good cry.

# CHOCOLATE IS MY MIDDLE NAME

Cynthia Blair

FAWCETT JUNIPER • NEW YORK

A Fawcett Juniper Book
Published by Ballantine Books
Copyright © 1992 by Cynthia Blair

All rights reserved under International and Pan-American
Copyright Conventions. Published in the United States by
Ballantine Books, a division of Random House, Inc., New
York, and simultaneously in Canada by Random House of
Canada Limited, Toronto.

Library of Congress Catalog Card Number: 91-93161

ISBN 0-449-70400-9

Manufactured in the United States of America

First Edition: September 1992

**To Emily Book**

To Nadine,

Best wishes,

*Cpi Blai*

# chapter
## one

"When you grow up, Carla, you should open a bakery!"

Eagerly Betsy Crane leaned across the kitchen table and grabbed another one of my world famous homemade specialties: dark chocolate fudge brownies marbled with sticky, gooey marshmallow. She rubbed her hands together greedily, brushed her headful of red-orange curls out of her eyes, and dug right in.

"Here, here," Samantha Langtree said with a nod. "I second the motion. You are without doubt the best brownie baker in the world."

As usual, she was much more polite about the way she helped herself to a third brownie. Sam wasn't one to swoop down on them and stuff them in her face as fast as humanly possible, the way Betsy and I were. Instead, she picked one up gently and then nibbled at the edge, as daintily as a princess at a tea party.

And then, her green eyes glowing, Betsy cried, "Hey, I have a great idea! How about opening up a stand at the Hanover Mall? I hear that new wing they're opening next week is going to have a food court. You could sell these marshmallow brownie things by the dozen. I can see it all now: Carla's Confections! Yum!'' As if to show just how popular they were bound to be, she popped a big chunk into her mouth.

I shrugged, trying to be modest. ''Well, thanks, Betsy, but I—''

''Yes,'' she went on, ''I think that's a real brainstorm. During the week, you could spend every night baking your head off—Samantha and I would help, of course—and then on the weekends you could sell everything you made. I bet you'd be a millionaire by Thanksgiving!'' Betsy paused to lick a clump of fudge off her thumb. ''And I know who would be your first customer.''

''Thanks for the compliment,'' I said with a grin. ''But the truth is, I'm not all that interested in baking for other people. Except you two, of course,'' I added quickly, wanting to make sure my two best pals in the entire universe knew just how much I appreciated their friendship, which was still pretty new to me. ''It's the eating part I enjoy, not the baking.''

''Too bad,'' Samantha said with a sigh. ''You've got a real talent, Carla.''

I shrugged once again. ''You know what I always say: chocolate is my middle name.''

That certainly was an understatement. And sitting around my kitchen table after school with my two friends, doing my part to help gobble up the little snack I'd whipped up the evening before, was only the beginning.

You see, practically my whole life, I've been madly in love with food.

When I was a kid, my favorite part of kindergarten wasn't fingerpainting or building with blocks or playing dress up or even listening to story hour . . . it was snack time. My fondest memories of going to amusement parks were not of the scary roller coaster or the fun house or the thrill of throwing balls at bottles and winning a giant pink teddy bear . . . they were of the cotton candy and the snow cones and the foot-long hot dogs my mom and dad always bought me. Birthday parties meant cake and ice cream, the Fourth of July meant hamburgers and toasted marshmallows, Halloween—the *best* holiday—meant all the chocolate I could eat.

The bad news, meanwhile, is that I've also had a lifelong battle with my weight.

Yes, my love of sweets and other goodies took its toll. Mainly around my middle, although I have to admit I'm pretty round all over. I was always the chubbiest girl at school, starting with Day One. You see, even back in kindergarten, those mid-morning picker-uppers of Oreos and apple juice had already begun to catch up with me. Even then, I was bigger than any of the other five-year-olds, even chunky Timmy Constable, the boy who could eat a whole box of animal crackers without once coming up for air.

It went on from there. All through elementary school, I was the plump kid in the class. My clothes were always two or three sizes bigger than everyone else's. In gym, I was the one who did the fewest number of sit-ups, who was the slowest in the relay races, who couldn't climb the ropes . . . who couldn't even get off the ground. The other girls would groan when I was assigned to their teams. When we all had lunch in the school cafeteria, I was the one who got teased—or made fun of, depending on how you wanted to look at it—whenever I finished everything on my plate.

I didn't like it, of course. Especially as I got older and that teasing became more and more common. From boys, especially. No, I guess you could even say I hated it. I dreaded gym day, I dreaded lunchtime, I *really* dreaded the day we got weighed and measured by the school nurse. But the truth of the matter was, I felt there was absolutely nothing in the world I could do about it.

As if my lifelong battle with my weight wasn't bad enough, I've also had a lifelong battle with my parents about my weight. Oh, not that I blame them. Not really. They just wanted the best for me. They wanted me to be a cute little girl with pigtails and pretty ruffled dresses—or at least pink and lavender sweatsuits. But that's not what they got.

Then, finally, they just couldn't take it anymore. Over the past summer, my mom and dad actually sent me to a fat camp.

Camp Breezy Pines. You know the type. It's one of those places you always see advertised in the back of fashion magazines, a sleepaway camp especially designed for chubby little girls whose parents have decided it's time to melt away the baby fat. The ads show girls playing tennis, riding horses, and laughing and singing and having the time of their lives.

What they *don't* show you is girls sneaking boxes of butter cookies into their bunks. Or six-packs of Milky Way bars. Or even girls sending away to those fancy mail-order places that sell chocolate-chip cookies for about three hundred dollars a pound.

At least, that was my experience.

To be fair, that was only one aspect of it. There was another whole part to going away to good old Camp Breezy Pines, one that involved my learning something very important about myself . . . but I'll save that for later.

"Speaking of the new wing of the mall," Samantha suddenly said, meanwhile taking another mouse-size bite of her brownie, "when exactly is it going to open?"

"The grand opening is Monday, just four days away," Betsy replied. "I read about it in the newspaper."

I nodded. "I heard it advertised on the radio. Besides the food court, they're opening something like twenty new stores. It should be pretty cool. And they'll probably have some great sales . . . maybe even give away free stuff. Want to go check it out next week?"

"Definitely," Betsy said. "I can't wait. How about you, Samantha?"

"Count me in. In fact, I'll ask my father to lend me the charge cards."

"Good," I said. "Then it's all settled. We'll go together, the three of us."

"Well, of *course* we'll go together," Betsy said earnestly. "After all, isn't that what the Bubble Gum Gang is all about?"

The Bubble Gum Gang . . . now, that was something new.

You see, another aspect of being the fattest kid in the class was that it didn't exactly make me Miss Popularity. I always figured I was the only kid in the world who had a hard time making friends and fitting in. But then I found out I was wrong.

A few weeks earlier, Betsy and Samantha and I had started seventh grade at Hanover Junior High. I think I speak for all three of us when I say that since we were all starting out in a brand new place—for Betsy, a *totally* new place, because she had just moved to Hanover the summer before, right after her parents got divorced—we were all feeling a little bit like fish out of water. And we all recognized that being in a new school, one that was huge since it brought together kids from several small elementary schools, gave us a chance to make some new friends.

Each one of us, it turned out, had a long history of being outsiders. I, of course, had spent much of my life living with labels like "thunder thighs" and "blubber." Shy, quiet, smart Betsy, meanwhile, had been pegged as the class brain—teacher's pet, egghead, geek, whatever was the popular term at the time.

And Samantha Langtree, who looks like somebody out of a picture book with her long, straight, blond Alice-in-Wonderland hair, comes from the wealthiest family in all of Hanover. She lives in a mansion, she eats quail and caviar and truffles the way most of us eat hot dogs and French fries, and she spends her vacations doing things like playing polo in the English countryside or waterskiing in the south of France. In short, she's not somebody the other kids can relate to all that easily.

Not that we're not all nice, friendly, ordinary twelve-year-olds. We are definitely that. Was it our fault that hardly anybody else ever realized that? Anyway, the point is that when we found each other somewhere around the first week or two of school and recognized that the three of us were kindred spirits, a terrific friendship sprang up.

We called ourselves the Bubble Gum Gang in honor of one of Betsy's favorite habits—chewing bubble gum. And we dedicated ourselves to helping each other, solving any mysteries that crossed our path, experiencing whatever adventures we could, and above all being good friends to one other.

I must admit, at that point the only mysterious thing in our lives was wondering how we were going to make it through Mr. Homer's first-period English class. He was one of those teachers who were very big on things like oral reports and special projects— Betsy's idea of fun, maybe, but not mine.

But I wasn't worried. Something was bound to come up. Besides, at the moment, I was enjoying sitting back and hanging out with my two best friends.

Just then, the back door opened and in strutted Miss Kelly Farrell. My sixteen-year-old sister has a way of carrying herself as if she owns the place—

any place—and today was no exception. As she came into the kitchen, I actually felt guilty, sitting there with my friends. It was as if, just by being in the same space as Kelly, I was doing something I wasn't supposed to be doing.

As usual, she looked like the cover girl for some fashion magazine. Her long hair was smooth and shiny, glinting in the September sunshine that was streaming through the windows. It was pulled up on one side with one of those big scrunchy things. One that happened to be orange.

I'd rather die than wear orange. Orange is for pumpkins. Or squash. Or . . . or oranges.

Or for tall skinny girls who can actually carry off wearing an orange oversized T-shirt, even one being worn over skin-tight stretchy purple leggings. And tall and skinny just happen to be excellent words for describing Kelly. In fact, you could even say that she looks like a model.

No plump body for her, no short, dark curly hair like mine that's about as memorable as a used dish-towel. Besides being willowy, she also has gorgeous chestnut brown hair. And she's pretty. I mean, *really* pretty. She doesn't even need any makeup to look terrific.

She's also one of the sweetest people you could ever meet, something that just about everybody in the galaxy has noticed. During half her waking hours, there's a telephone sticking out of her ear. During three-quarters of that time, there's a boy at the other end.

Kelly and I have very little in common. She'd

rather blow dry her hair than eat dessert. She'd spend her last dollar on a new barrette instead of on a chocolate ice-cream cone. Her idea of a well-balanced breakfast is three gulps of orange juice.

It's hard to believe the two of us are related.

"Oh, *hi*," Kelly said, looking surprised. She blinked her big blue eyes a few times.

Maybe I was a little paranoid or something, but I immediately figured that what she was so puzzled about was the fact that her little sister—her unpopular sister—was hanging out with friends. And not one but two.

Or maybe it was just that she was tuning back in from her own little world, where everything always seemed to go exactly the way she wanted it to go.

"Hi, Kelly," I said. "Samantha, Betsy, this is my sister, Kelly."

"Hi," everybody said.

"Want a brownie?" Betsy said cheerfully. "Carla made them. They're fantastic."

Kelly glanced over at the table with a little frown. Brownies, I knew, were not exactly her thing.

"No, thanks. Actually, I've got to dash out again." She glanced at the small mirror stuck on the front of the refrigerator—her idea—and shook her head hard, as if she expected her hair to fall magically into place. Oddly enough, it did.

"Where are you going?" I asked. It was a funny thing. I thought I had decided that three brownies were enough. But suddenly there I was, staring at the plate, wondering whether or not I should help myself to another.

"I've got a job interview."

"A job interview! Doing what? Where?" I asked.

"It's over at the Hanover Mall. Have you heard that the new wing is opening up next week?"

"We certainly have!" Betsy said excitedly. "In fact, we were just talking about it."

"That's right," Samantha said with a nod. "We plan to check it out the first chance we get."

"Well, I not only want to check it out. They're opening a branch of my favorite clothing store and I intend to get a job there. It's called Clothes Circuit. I want to work there two or three afternoons a week, after school, plus Saturdays."

Betsy's eyes grew wide. "I know that place! Don't they sell really trendy clothes in outrageous colors?"

Kelly nodded. "They call that section the Neon Niche. They have other stuff, too. Really, though, the whole place is totally awesome. It's my favorite place to buy clothes in the world."

"That sounds very exciting," Samantha said.

"I'll say," Betsy agreed.

I, meanwhile, kept my eyes down. As far as I was concerned, this was just one more example of Kelly getting anything she wanted. It *figured* that she'd end up landing a job at her favorite store, the coolest one at the mall.

Almost as if she had been reading my mind, she said, "Of course, I don't have the job yet. I'm supposed to go over and talk to a man named Mr. Deegan in about an hour."

"Oh, you'll probably get it," Samantha said, trying to be encouraging. "I'm sure they need people, and since it's clear that you're enthusiastic about the place, this Mr. Deegan would be crazy not to hire you.''

"I hope so. I'd love the chance to make some real money. And of course I'd adore being able to work around such great clothes. I'd probably learn a lot about the fashion industry—not to mention the ins and outs of running a store. And there's one more thing," she added dreamily, checking herself in the mirror again. "It's a great way to meet new people.''

By that, I knew, Kelly meant new *boys*. Even working in a shop that sold clothes for the female half of the population, she would no doubt find a way of meeting more boys than there were at West Point. While the payoff of my hobby—baking—was delicious, mouth-watering treats, the payoff of Kelly's hobby—making herself look good—was the attention of boys.

"Too bad you girls are too young to work there," she went on. "But then again, you'll get your chance some day, after you're finished with junior high.''

The way she said "junior high" made it sound like the state prison or something.

And then, all of a sudden, her voice got soft. She came over and put her hand on my shoulder. "You know, I was thinking, Carla. Getting a job like this sounds like something you would enjoy, once you get to be old enough. It might be good for you. A chance to have some fun, to do something different . . . to get out a little bit.''

That was so like Kelly. Just when I was all set to resent her for being beautiful, popular, poised, totally *cool*—in short, everything I wasn't—she acted like this really sweet, considerate big sister. And I was left not knowing *how* to feel.

"Working in a store does sound like it could be interesting," Samantha commented. I was sure she was only trying to be polite.

"I'm not so sure about that," Betsy countered. "I mean, it does sound like it might be kind of fun. But during the school year? When do you expect to find time to do your homework?"

Kelly frowned. "I've been waiting for somebody to ask me that."

"You mean somebody like Mom and Dad," I said, picking up on what she was thinking.

"Exactly. I don't expect them to be too crazy about the idea. But I really, really want to do this. It's my big chance to make some money." Thoughtfully, she added, "I desperately need to buy some new clothes."

Right, I was thinking. Just as desperately as the state of Alaska needs more snow.

"Anyway, Carla, I was kind of hoping you'd do me a favor."

"What is it?"

Kelly looked at me with puppy dog eyes. "Could you please, please, *please* not mention this to Mom and Dad? I want to be the one to break the news to them, and not until after I know whether or not I actually have the job. Please, Carla?"

It was all I could do to keep from throwing her a bone.

"Sure, Kelly. I won't say a word."

"Good. I knew I could count on you."

Already her mind seemed to be elsewhere. She opened the refrigerator, took out a can of diet soda, and headed toward the back door. "If anyone wonders where I am, just tell them I'll be back by dinner time."

And she was gone.

"She seems nice," said Betsy, gesturing toward the back door with her chin.

"Very nice," Samantha agreed. "Very pretty, too."

Betsy was nodding. "Yeah, I'll bet she's really popular at school."

"Yeah, I guess so." There I was, staring at that plate of brownies once again.

Our conversation quickly turned to other topics. Mainly, which clubs we were going to go out for now that the school year was starting to get underway. Betsy was thinking about the school newspaper. Samantha was considering the art club.

I, meanwhile, was simply glad we weren't still talking about my sister. Or, for that matter, the new wing over at the shopping mall. I had been looking forward to going to the Hanover Mall with my friends, and now, all of a sudden, I was losing interest. It was as if the whole mall now belonged to my sister. The idea of having fun there was tainted by the fact that *she* was going to be part of it.

At that point, I wasn't even sure if I wanted to go anymore. And so it never occurred to me, not even for a zillionth of a second, that the opening of this new bunch of stores—and especially Kelly's interest in getting a job at one of them—was going to turn out to be the single most significant event of my entire life.

# chapter
## two

I was sitting in homeroom the following morning, only half awake, when the announcement came over the loudspeaker. The fact that Hanover Junior High School's drama club was getting geared up to put on a play was mentioned in this really casual way. Actually, some kids could have even missed it completely, given the way it was thrown in somewhere between a warning for faculty members not to park in the west parking lot and a correction for that day's lunch menu.

Normally, something like pizza being substituted for tuna fish sandwiches would have been of great interest to me. But as soon as the next announcement was made, I forgot all about the lure of mozzarella cheese.

"The drama club will hold its first meeting of the year after school today, in the auditorium. Ms. Hart, the club's adviser, says that anyone interested in trying out for this semester's production of *Our Town* should come to the meeting to pick up a script."

All of a sudden, nothing else mattered. Not the

fact that it was raining, not the fact that there were rumors of a surprise quiz coming up in math class, not even the fact that I had spent most of the night before brooding about Kelly having gotten her dream job at Clothes Circuit over at the new mall.

A play. The drama club was putting on a play.

And anyone was welcome to audition.

I guess this is as good a time as any to go back to my summer at Camp Breezy Pines. That place was very big on building up a girl's confidence. The people who ran it had some weird philosophy about overeating being related to the way kids felt about themselves.

Anyway, that was where the water-skiing and the horseback riding and the tennis came in. Sure, it was partly to burn up calories and teach us about the joys and wonders of getting up out of a chair and moving around. And the camp counselors' insistence upon forcing us to try new things, whether we wanted to or not, was designed to help us discover fun activities that had never before occurred to us to try.

But they were also trying to build up our confidence. I think the way they thought was, if you're the kind of girl who's always hanging around in the background, trying not to be noticed, and then you discover that you have this unexpected talent for—I don't know—throwing horseshoes or something, it will suddenly, magically, make you feel better about yourself.

I didn't buy it. Not for a minute.

That is, until the camp counselors forced me to be in a play.

It was a musical. Actually, it was what they call light opera. *H.M.S. Pinafore* was the name, and it had been written by this really famous team named Gilbert and Sullivan.

Under normal circumstances, I never would have tried something like that, not in a million years. But as I've already said, we weren't talking normal circumstances. I mean, it's not like I had any real choice in the matter or anything. They *made* me do it. And the really incredible part was that it turned out that I enjoyed it. Loved it, even.

The even *more* incredible part was that I turned out to be *good* at it.

I sang. I danced. I acted. And, at the risk of sounding a little bit like a show-off, I am pleased to report that the audience loved me.

The other kids at the camp all saw it, of course, and so did the counselors. The kids' parents were also there, since we put it on during Parents' Weekend. And the one thing that everybody seemed to agree on was that I was the best thing about the entire show.

*Me!*

Chubby, quiet, hide-in-the-background, blend-in-with-the-wallpaper Carla Farrell!

It was a pretty amazing experience, discovering that I had this special talent that I had never, ever suspected I had—not in my wildest, craziest dreams. In fact, I was still marveling over it, even now when the summer was over and that part of it, Parents' Weekend, was nothing more than a wonderful memory that I played over and over again in my mind, saving it for special, private moments like before I went to sleep at night.

And now, here, totally out of the blue, was the chance to do it all over again.

I could hardly wait for homeroom to be over and first-period English to begin. Both Samantha and Betsy were in that class with me, and I was so eager to tell them the good news that I was positively bursting at the seams.

"Betsy! Samantha!" I cried, bursting into Room 201, Mr. Homer's classroom. "Did you hear it? Did you hear the announcement?"

My two friends looked up at me in confusion, leaving the conversation they had been having in midair. Fortunately, Mr. Homer tends to be a little out of it a lot of the time—he's not what you'd call a morning person—and so our English class always gets started a couple of minutes late. At the moment, he was standing in the back of the room discussing this year's football team with Jason Downing, the blond, blue-eyed, gorgeous captain of Hanover Junior High's team.

"Yes, I heard the announcements," Betsy said, looking a little confused. "And to be perfectly honest, Carla, I don't think that having pizza for lunch instead of tuna fish sandwiches is all *that* exciting."

"No, no, not *that* announcement," I said impatiently, waving my hands in the air. "The *other* one. The one about the school play."

"Oh, yes, *that* one," said Samantha. "The drama club is putting on *Our Town*. It sounds like fun. Let's all go see it together, all right?"

"I don't want to see it," I cried. "I want to be *in* it!"

It was only then that I realized I had never told Betsy and Samantha about my experience at Camp Breezy Pines. Oh, I had mentioned it once in class, back on the very first day of school when we all had to stand up, one at a time, and talk about how we'd spent our summer vacation.

But I had never had the chance to tell them how much it had meant to me. How I loved being on the stage, acting in front of an audience, becoming another person—even someone who was totally different from the way I really was. And I had never had the chance to tell them how *good* I was at it.

Smugly, I thought to myself, Betsy and Samantha and everybody else in town will be finding that out for themselves soon enough!

Out loud, I said, "Listen, this will probably come pretty much as news to you both, but acting happens to be something I've kind of got a real knack for. And not only am I going to try out for this play, I intend to get the lead!"

"The lead?" Betsy repeated, her mouth dropping open.

"That's right," I said firmly. "I'm going to play the part of Emily Webb."

Just then, Mr. Homer remembered that there were other things in life besides football. Much more important and interesting things, in fact . . . like the comma.

"All right, class," he was saying, striding up to the front of the room. "Let's take out our grammar

textbooks. Today we're going to tackle that comma—
if you'll excuse the reference to football.''

Most of the class groaned. Mr. Homer puts a lot
of energy into trying to be funny. He really does
mean well, I suppose, but most of the time his jokes
never get off the ground.

Not that it mattered very much, at least not to me.
After all, I was hardly listening. I was too busy
imagining how it was going to feel playing Emily
Webb, the pretty young woman who was the most
important character in Thornton Wilder's play, *Our
Town*.

I mean, how could I be expected to concentrate
on the comma when all of a sudden I was *this* close
to being a star?

I half expected that three-quarters of the school
would show up at that afternoon's meeting of the
drama club. I pictured them swarming through the
doors of the auditorium, pushing and shoving, demanding copies of the script, each one of them eager
to be a star.

So I was kind of relieved when I slipped into the
school auditorium immediately after the end of the
last period that Friday and found only a handful of
people sitting there. Most of them were sprinkled
throughout the first four or five rows, looking up at
the stage expectantly even though the only thing going on up there was that a little more dust was ac-
cumulating.

I sat behind all of them, somewhere in the middle
of row eight. That way, I figured, I could see what

was going on without actually being seen myself. You know, the old fly-on-the-wall routine.

There were six or seven boys there. Frankly, I wasn't particularly interested in the male would-be actors. After all, they weren't my competition. Instead, I immediately turned my attention to the girls—the *other* contenders for the role of Emily Webb, the role I was already thinking about as *my* role.

I was encouraged by what I saw. There were maybe eight or ten other girls there, and none of them seemed to be taking any of this very seriously. At least, if the way they were behaving was any sign. Mostly they were sitting together in clusters of twos or threes, chatting and giggling and acting as if being there were no big deal.

I sat back in my seat and breathed a sigh of relief. So far, so good. I started to get comfortable, figuring I'd have to wait a while for things to get underway. But I had barely found a place to tuck my schoolbooks when a woman I had never seen before—presumably a teacher, presumably Ms. Hart—climbed up the stairs and stood right smack in the middle of the stage.

"Good afternoon, boys and girls. I'd like to thank you for coming today," began the tall, pretty woman.

She was wearing a simple dress, a rich emerald green color, with a green and blue scarf tied around her neck. She looked very worldly. In fact, she looked kind of like a grown-up version of my sister Kelly.

"My name is Ms. Hart, and I'm the adviser for

the drama club. As I'm sure most of you already know, we're going to be performing Thornton Wilder's famous work *Our Town*. It is, I might add, one of my favorite plays. It's scheduled to be put on in just six short weeks, so we've really got our work cut out for us.''

No sweat, I was thinking, settling back in my chair and folding my arms across my chest. Ms. Hart, you're dealing with a pro. If anybody can perfect the part of Emily Webb in six short weeks, it's yours truly.

''Now I'd like to begin by handing out a copy of the script to each of you. That way, you can begin familiarizing yourselves with the play. You can also start thinking about which roles you'd like to try out for.''

Already a hand shot up. It was one of the gigglers, sitting right in front.

''Ms. Hart,'' the girl asked in a voice that even I could tell was much too whiny ever to play the part of Emily, ''what happens if you try out for a part, and even though you do a pretty good job, you still don't get it? Does that mean you're automatically out of the play?''

It was a good question; I had to admit that.

''No,'' Ms. Hart replied. ''In that case, I will assign you a part, one that I think you're right for, based on your reading.''

''What's a reading?'' the same girl asked.

I rolled my eyes upward.

This club *needs* me, I was thinking. Just let me at that script.

Ms. Hart was much more patient. "During the audition, you'll be standing up here on the stage, reading some of the lines from the script. The idea is for you to show me how well you can act. You'll be expected not only to read from the script, but to act as much like the character as you can. That's called a reading."

I'm ready, I'm ready, I was thinking.

"When are the auditions?" asked the girl's friend, a fellow giggler.

"This Monday," said Ms. Hart.

"Monday!" some of us gasped.

"That's only three days away!" cried giggler number two.

"Yes, I know it doesn't give you very much time," Ms. Hart said. "But remember that we don't *have* very much time. Three days should give you enough time to look over the script, decide which part you'd most like to play, and pick out a passage and practice it. It's not as if you have to memorize it. At least, not yet."

I, of course, already knew all about this routine. At Camp Breezy Pines, we had been given the scripts and then made to read from them on the spot. It turned out to be a good thing, too, since that way, none of us had a chance to get nervous. It was that reading that got me the lead in *Pinafore*.

Still, three days was not a lot of time if you really wanted to master a part. I was going to have to dedicate most of the weekend to preparing for my stage debut here at Hanover Junior High. It would be hard work.

Even so, I was feeling pretty confident as Ms. Hart gave a little talk about how the production would also need people to do behind-the-scenes work—lighting and costumes, for example. In fact, I was so busy planning out my strategy that I was hardly listening.

Then she came down off the stage and started handing out the scripts. How excited I was when my copy was passed back to me! This was it, my big chance. I was going to star in this production. I was going to show everybody just who Carla Farrell really was . . . and what she could do. This, for me, was going to be a whole new beginning.

I was trying to decide what to bake for an after-school celebration of this new development in my life—brownies again? or maybe something a little more daring, like a chocolate mousse?—when the side door of the auditorium suddenly opened. Everyone looked over. We couldn't help it, because those doors are very, very noisy—and whoever was coming in was very, very late.

I froze.

Standing in the doorway was Wendy Lipton.

Wendy Lipton, one of the most popular girls at school. Thin, blond, the envy of just about everyone. And as if she didn't already have it all, she had just tried out for the cheerleading squad and had been awarded the position of head cheerleader.

Maybe she's lost, I thought. Or maybe she's looking for one of her friends.

But before I had a chance to come up with another possible, if unlikely, reason for her to be here in the auditorium on this particular Friday afternoon,

Wendy swung her long hair back over her shoulders and asked, "Is this where the drama club is meeting?"

Don't worry about it, I was thinking as I watched her prance over to Ms. Hart and pick up a copy of the script. She'll never get the part of Emily. *I'm* the one who's such a good actress. *I'm* the one who has had experience. I *know* I can do it better than Wendy. I refused to let her appearance on the scene get in the way of my enthusiasm.

In fact, I was determined to do my best to forget all about her. Already I was reading through the script, picking out the lines that belonged to Emily.

By Monday, I intended to know this character better than I knew myself. I would work harder on learning this script than I had ever worked on anything else my entire life. I would eat, sleep, and breathe Emily Webb.

In fact, by Monday, I intended to *be* Emily Webb, if that was what it was going to take to get this part.

# chapter
## three

The second I got home from school that afternoon, I was on the phone. First I called Betsy.

"How did the drama club meeting go?" she asked right off.

I really appreciated her being so in tune with what was on my mind.

"It was great," I reported back. "The club's adviser, Ms. Hart, handed out the scripts on the spot, since we only have six weeks to get the play ready."

"That's exciting! When are the auditions being held?"

"This Monday."

"This Monday! That's only three days away!"

"I know. But I've promised myself to have learned everything I can about the part of Emily Webb by then. Besides, I have the whole weekend to get ready."

There was a long pause. "Carla," Betsy said, "is the part of Emily the only one you intend to try out for?"

"It's certainly the one I want—and, I might add,

the one I have every intention of getting," I told her confidently. "The way it works, though, is that if for some reason some of the kids don't get the exact part they want, there's a good chance they'll be assigned some other role."

"Well, *that's* good," she said. Quickly, she added, "For all the other kids, I mean."

For the first time since I had heard about the play, I felt a little bit nervous about what the outcome was going to be. "You . . . you do think it's a good idea to try out for the part of Emily Webb, don't you?"

"If that's what you want, Carla, then go for it!" she cried. "Besides, I just know you'll make the most terrific Emily Webb in history."

I guess that's what friends are for, I was thinking as I hung up and dialed Samantha's number.

"You'll come see the play, won't you?" I asked after I had filled her in on all the details of the drama club meeting and my own intention of dedicating my entire existence to turning myself into Emily Webb over the next three days.

"Are you kidding?" she cried. "I'll get my father to videotape the whole thing! And maybe, afterward, my parents will throw a party for you and the entire cast—"

"Whoa! Slow down!" I said, laughing. "Just promise me you'll show up, okay?"

"I'll be in the front row. I promise!"

I was still on Cloud Nine at dinner time. I couldn't wait to tell my family my good news. But I decided to wait for just the right moment.

That turned out to be a good thing. Kelly, as usual,

managed to put herself right in the center of things even before we had finished our salads.

"Mom? Dad? There's, uh, something I've been meaning to talk to you about."

My parents both looked up from their lettuce and cucumbers with Thousand Island dressing. There was a definite nervousness to Kelly's tone, and their superhuman powers of hearing, something all parents possess, had picked up on it right away.

"Yes, honey?" my mom said encouragingly. "What is it?"

Kelly was playing with her salad, watching her cucumbers slide around in the dressing, as absorbed as if she were glued to a tennis match. "You know how you're both always talking about how important it is for kids my age to learn responsibility? Taking care of themselves, acting grown-up, learning how to manage money, things like that?"

My father nodded. "All of those are extremely important, Kelly."

She smiled. Then she looked up, putting aside both her fork and her fascination with green leafy vegetables. "I was hoping you'd say that. Because I'm pleased to announce that I have found the perfect way to master all of those."

"Really?" my mother said. "My goodness. I can hardly wait to hear what you've got up your sleeve."

My sister hesitated. I got the feeling she was trying to decide how to spring the big news. All at once, sort of like an avalanche, where you sit back and hope for the best? Or gradually, trying the gentle approach? It was clear which one won.

"I got a part-time job at one of the new stores over at the mall. I start Monday after school."

All of a sudden, salad was the very last thing on anybody's mind.

"A job?" my mother cried.

"A job?" demanded my father.

"I guess we're all pretty clear on that one," I mumbled.

"Kelly, we have told you again and again that we don't think it's a good idea for you to work during the school year," my father sputtered.

"That's right," my mother agreed. "You should be using your free time to be doing homework, not working at some part-time job."

"Especially at the mall!" my dad said.

"Please, let me tell my side of it," Kelly pleaded.

My parents both nodded. I knew they would listen to Kelly. They always did.

"First of all, I really do think that working a few hours a week will help me learn things like responsibility and money management. Second, you two are always on my case about my asking for money for new clothes and CDs and movies and all that. This way, I would be able to earn my own money, and I could quit bugging you. Third, the job I got is at this really cool store, the type of place I've always wanted to work. . . ."

"So you already have this job?" My father was trying to sound stern, but I could tell he was weakening. Once again, I was seeing that no one who was made of flesh and blood was capable of saying no to Kelly Farrell. Robots, maybe. But not living, breathing human beings.

Kelly nodded. ''Mr. Deegan said I was clearly the best of the applicants that he'd talked to. And more than a dozen girls applied for the job!''

''It's nice that you did so well at your interview,'' my mother observed. In about thirty seconds flat, she had gone from sounding dismayed to sounding proud.

''Anyway, I knew you wouldn't be crazy about the idea,'' Kelly continued, ''so I came up with kind of a plan. How about if I try working at Clothes Circuit for a month? Then we can all sit down and talk about how it's going. How I'm doing in school, whether I'm getting all my homework done, that kind of thing.''

My parents looked at each other. My mother shrugged. Inwardly, I groaned.

''Well, I suppose we could try it—for a month, that is,'' Mom said.

''But you had better make sure your schoolwork doesn't suffer,'' my father said, wagging a finger at Kelly. ''If that job of yours gets in the way of home-work and studying even the slightest bit—''

''I know, I know,'' Kelly said happily. ''But be-lieve me, Daddy, I'm not going to let that happen!''

I glanced over at my mother. She was beaming as brightly as the moon on Halloween night.

''Actually, Kelly,'' she said, ''I'm kind of proud of you. You showed a lot of initiative, going out and getting this job for yourself.''

"Of course, we would have appreciated it if you had talked to us first," my father interjected.

"Oh, of course," my mother said. "But even so . . ."

I was beginning to wonder how I was going to stomach the rest of my dinner. I decided it was time to change the topic of conversation to something more interesting, something relevant to everyone . . . something like my own recent accomplishments.

"Kelly isn't the only one in this family who's moving on to bigger and better things," I said, trying to sound casual.

My parents both looked over at me.

Kelly, meanwhile, said, "What on earth are you talking about, Carla?"

"Oh, just the school play. The one the drama club is going to put on." Meaningfully, I added, "The play that I'm going to star in."

"You? The star?" Kelly's mouth had dropped open. "That's fantastic!"

"Congratulations, honey," my mother said warmly.

"That's great news," my father said. "And hardly surprising, after that terrific performance you gave at Camp Breezy Pines a few weeks ago. Is this going to be another musical?"

"Uh, no. Actually, it's *Our Town*. You know, by Thornton Wilder." For a minute there, I had been feeling ten feet tall. But already I could feel myself shrinking back down to normal size. "And, uh, I don't actually have the part of Emily yet. But don't worry about that little detail. Auditions are being held on Monday. And I have no doubt that I'm going to be the best one. I'm a natural to play Emily Webb!''

I pretended not to notice when my parents exchanged those worried, knowing looks that parents are always exchanging. Instead, I concentrated on what Kelly was saying.

''You've got a great chance at that part, Sis. Dad is right. You really did steal the show at Breezy Pines. The day of the auditions, just go out there and knock 'em dead!''

Now that I had told half the world about my intention of starring in the school play—not only Betsy and Samantha, but my parents and Kelly as well—I had no choice but to throw myself into learning the part of Emily. That very evening, right after dinner, I was going to have to turn all my attention to the script, throwing myself into it with my heart and soul.

After all, if a star was going to be born, first I was going to have to go through a few labor pains.

It was one of those cool September evenings. Indian Summer that time of year is called, the time when you'd be stretching the truth if you said it was autumn, but you could hardly call what was going on summer. It was the kind of evening that has a special feeling all its own. But I had no time for mooning around. I had some serious work to do, and so I headed for one of the very best spots in the world: my old swing set.

Not that I play on it anymore. I'm much too grown-up for that. Slides and swings, after all, are kid stuff. Even so, I still love hanging out there, sitting on what used to be my favorite swing, a wooden one that I swear has taken on the shape of my bottom over the years. I've spent a lot of time there, just thinking or daydreaming or—like this time—reading.

I started on page one of the *Our Town* script and went all the way through. It didn't take me all that long. That's a funny thing about reading plays: there's so much space between the lines that each person speaks that it makes for quick reading. It might take two hours to watch a play being performed, but reading through it goes much faster than that.

I was just about to go back to the beginning, to start going over and over the lines belonging to Emily Webb, when I heard a rustle in the bushes. My first thought was that it must be Kelly, teasing me. I looked up, scowling, ready to complain.

But the next thing I knew, I heard a familiar voice saying, "Now really, Carla. Is *that* the way the character of Emily Webb would sit on a swing?"

"Betsy!" I cried. "What are you doing here?"

"Actually, coming here wasn't my idea," she explained, walking around the side of the house. "It was *hers*."

And there was Samantha, not far behind.

"Hi, Carla," she said, waving. "How's it going?"

I was totally flabbergastaed. "What are you two *doing* here? I thought you'd be out doing something fun while I was stuck here on a Friday night, studying my part for the auditions on Monday."

"We *are* doing something fun." Samantha sat down on the swing next to me. "We've come over to help you."

"That's right," Betsy agreed, draping herself across the slide. "Isn't that what the Bubble Gum Gang is all about? Helping one other?"

Samantha was nodding. "Just tell us what to do. Assign each of us a part, and we'll read through the play with you."

My mouth had dropped open so far it was a wonder I didn't get any gravel in it. "You two are going to do that for me?"

"Of course," Betsy said. "Now give us the background on the play."

"Right. Take it from the top. Tell us the whole story."

So I did. *Our Town* is a play that celebrates the wonders of ordinary, day-to-day life, as lived by ordinary, day-to-day people. It's a reminder to the audience that life is precious . . . and so are the people around us. It takes place in this really cool, old-fashioned New England town around the turn of the century.

The part I wanted to play, Emily Webb, was a young woman. A lot of the action is seen through her eyes. She's really pretty central to the whole thing, since in Act One she becomes engaged, in Act Two she gets married, and in Act Three she comes back as a ghost to look back and realize that she was so busy *living* her life that she never took the time to step back and *appreciate* it.

"I think I've got it," Samantha said when I was

finished. "Emily Webb is sort of the main character, then. She's the one who's pretty and sweet and innocent. She's the one the audience is supposed to identify with."

"She's also the one who goes through the most changes," Betsy added. As usual, being such a brain, she was able to see a little bit more than the rest of us.

"Exactly," I told them. "It's the most important part in the play. And that's why it's the part I'm trying out for."

"Sure. It makes sense that you'd want the lead," Betsy said. "Now what about some of these other parts? Like Mrs. Webb, for example? Isn't she Emily's mother?"

"You've got it. That's what we call a character part," I explained. "It's a strong, interesting part, but it's not like being the star. Mrs. Webb is an older woman. It's the kind of role that's fun to play, I guess, but it's not like being the focus of the whole play."

"Gee, that's funny. That sounds like the kind of role I think I'd want to play," Betsy said wistfully. "That is, if I were the type of person who had the courage to go on the stage in the first place."

"But Carla wants the lead," Samantha insisted. "And that's the part we're going to help her get."

"Well, then," Betsy said with a grin, "what are we waiting for?"

For the next several hours, Betsy and Samantha and I practiced acting out the play. When the sun started to go down and it got chilly, we went inside, to my bedroom. As we sat on the floor, devouring a big bowl of potato chips, we kept on working. In fact, we worked and worked until my head was so full of the play that I thought I really *was* Emily Webb.

"Stop!" I finally cried. "Enough! I can't take any more!"

Betsy glanced over at the clock I keep next to my bed.

"Wow!" she cried. "It's already past ten o'clock! I've got to get home!"

"Me, too," said Samantha. "Gee, I was having so much fun that I didn't even notice it was getting so late. You know, I'm kind of enjoying this play business."

By that point, I was soaring. I really had the part of Emily down well, thanks to my two pals. And I still had the rest of the weekend to study it. I was totally confident that by Monday, I was going to be the best darned Emily that anyone had ever seen.

"Would it make you nervous if Betsy and I came to the audition?" Samantha asked as I was walking my friends to the door.

"We'd sit way in the back of the auditorium," Betsy added anxiously. "I mean, we wouldn't want to distract you or anything."

"I'd be *honored* if you would come," I told them. "I won't be nervous at all. Oh, sure, maybe I'll get a few butterflies in my stomach beforehand. But once I'm up there on that stage, I *become* the character I'm playing. I won't even remember that you're out there. I'll be too busy being Emily Webb."

"Well, then, we've got a date!" Betsy said firmly. "Monday, the auditorium, three o'clock sharp."

"Good luck," Samantha called over her shoulder as she and Betsy walked out into the cool night. "Or as they say in show biz, 'break a leg!' "

I expected that our long evening of concentrating would have worn me out. But once I was in bed, I couldn't sleep at all. My heart was pounding, and I was so energetic that I felt like I could run a marathon.

When Ms. Hart had first told us that the auditions for *Our Town* would be held on Monday, it had seemed so close. Now that I was ready, however, it seemed much too far away. I wondered how I would ever survive until then.

Finally, in the middle of running through Emily's lines over and over again in my head, I fell asleep. But for all the rest I got, I might as well have stayed awake. All that night, I kept dreaming that I was part of the cast of *Our Town*, and that it was opening night of the play.

Needless to say, my portrayal of Emily was the hit of the show.

# chapter
## four

I was beginning to think that Monday was never going to roll around. Surprise, surprise: it finally did.

The only thing that mattered, the only thing there was room for in my mind, was the audition. The fact that it was pouring rain—again—didn't bother me a bit. At breakfast, I barely noticed that my mother was wearing a brand new outfit. I kept forgetting that there was a history quiz scheduled for that afternoon.

Surprisingly enough, I wasn't nervous. I was more what you'd call excited. I couldn't wait to prove what I could do up there on that stage. And now, it was only a matter of hours before I had the chance to do what I did best. I don't know how I got through that day. But, like always, somehow I managed.

I went into the auditorium at three o'clock, right after the last bell. My hair was freshly combed, and my face was all flushed. Betsy and Samantha were already there. I spotted them sitting in the back, far away from the action—but still *there* for me.

I was glad they had come. Somehow, having them

in the audience, cheering me on, was going to make the whole thing that much easier.

I, meanwhile, took a seat in the third row. When the sign-up sheet that was being passed around got to me, I signed in. My name was way at the bottom.

Then I sat back and took a look around. I was anxious to check out who else was there, ready to strut their stuff. I discovered that the same kids were there, more or less, that had been there the Friday before for the drama club's first meeting. The "more" part was that there were a few new faces sitting in the audience. The "less" part was that one or two of the ninth graders hadn't bothered to show up this time.

Then Wendy came in, surrounded by three of her friends. I grimaced when I saw her adoring fan club, but of course they didn't notice me. They were all too busy fawning over Wendy, telling her how terrific she was going to be, insisting that she shouldn't be nervous at all because she was guaranteed to be the best.

I could hardly wait to show them what "the best" meant.

"Okay, everybody, let's get started," said Ms. Hart, getting up from her seat in the front row and turning around to face the two dozen or so people sprinkled throughout the first eight or nine rows of the auditorium. "Once again, I'd like to thank you for coming—and for being such good sports about getting ready for this audition on such short notice. I'm going to be calling you to read one at a time, based on the order in which you signed in.

"That means our first victim will be . . ." She squinted in the dim light of the auditorium, peering at the sign-up sheet she had balanced on top of her copy of the script. "Marilyn Gates."

Since I was near the end of the list, I got to see almost everyone else audition before my turn came up. The performances varied a lot. Some of the readings were pretty bad. Some, I was surprised to see, were actually terrific.

One boy in particular, Andrew Morris, had tremendous stage presence. He spoke clearly, in a nice loud voice, and his mannerisms were very natural. He was reading the longest role in the whole play, the only one that was more visible than the role of Emily Webb: the Stage Manager. There was no doubt in my mind that he would get the part.

Finally, it was my turn.

"Carla Farrell," Ms. Hart called. "You're up next."

I wasn't the least bit nervous. In fact, I was the very picture of confidence as I strutted up onto the stage.

"Carla Farrell?" Ms. Hart called from her seat in the front row.

"That's me." I made a point of speaking loudly and clearly. It's never too soon to start making a good impression, I always say.

"What grade are you in, Carla?"

"Seventh."

"Do you have any acting experience?"

"Oh, yes!" I cried. "This past summer, I went to camp, and . . ."

From somewhere in the auditorium came the distinct sound of laughter. Giggles, to be exact. I could feel my face turning red. It seemed as if everybody in the entire school knew that I had gone to fat camp that summer. Well, I'll show them, I was thinking. I did a lot more than learn about substituting fruit for sweet snacks and eating a well-balanced breakfast. I learned how to *act*.

"Anyway," I went on after taking a deep breath, "this past summer, I starred in a production of *H.M.S. Pinafore*."

Ms. Hart, at least, was impressed.

"Really? Then you must be able to sing, as well."

"I can sing, and I can even dance a little," I reported proudly.

More laughter. This time, I didn't turn red. Instead, I simply made up my mind that I was going to show these turkeys a thing or two.

"Which part are you going to be reading for today?" Ms. Hart asked pleasantly.

"Emily Webb," I said. "And, uh, I won't be reading it. I memorized it."

"You *memorized* it?"

"Well, not the *whole* thing." Suddenly I was afraid of appearing overly anxious. "Just the part where she comes back from being dead and chooses the one day she wants to relive: her twelfth birthday."

"My goodness, Carla. You've certainly done your homework." Ms. Hart sounded more impressed than ever.

I was tempted to tell her how much being in this

production meant to me, to let her know how badly I wanted the part of Emily. But I decided to try playing it safe. I just gave a little nod.

"Let's get started, then. I'll read all the other parts." In the dim light of the auditorium, I could see Ms. Hart opening up her copy of the script.

"It begins on page sixty-two," I offered, trying to be helpful. I wanted to show her just how cooperative I could be.

"Fine. Why don't we start where Emily says 'Hello'?"

I nodded. Then, I folded my hands in front of me, took two deep breaths, and closed my eyes. It was all slipping away: the auditorium, Ms. Hart, the other kids, even the monsters who had been giggling in back.

When I opened up my eyes, I *was* Emily Webb.

"Hello," I began in a voice that wasn't quite mine.

"Hello, Emily," Ms. Hart echoed, reciting the next line in the play, one that belonged to a character named Mrs. Soames.

I don't really remember all that much about what happened over the next five minutes or so. All I know is that I could feel that I was making each line, each *word*, come alive. It wasn't what I was saying; it was what Emily was saying.

And then, suddenly, I heard a voice that didn't belong, one that didn't fit. It was Ms. Hart—sounding like Ms. Hart, not Mrs. Soames or Mrs. Gibbs or any of the other characters.

"Thank you, Carla," she said.

I was so startled that I jumped.

"You did a fine job. Thank you."

I stood on the stage for few seconds longer, trying to get my bearings. I could feel a certain tension in the auditorium. The room was silent, but it was as if something strange—something wonderful, something special—was lingering in the air, like the sweet smell of lilacs on a warm day in May.

I knew what it was. It was the awe, the *respect*, I had earned from the people in the audience. They recognized what had just happened. They knew that, for the few minutes I had been up there on the stage, I had become Emily.

I was wearing a big, sloppy grin as I walked off the stage. I couldn't help it. There's nothing like knowing you've done a fantastic job at something, that you've been the very best you could ever be, to make you feel giddy.

"You were *incredible*!" Betsy whispered the moment I had sat down in the auditorium once again. She and Samantha had tiptoed up the aisle, coming over to me from where they'd been sitting in back. Now they were behind me, leaning forward to whisper their enthusiastic praise.

"That was really something," Samantha agreed. "You know, Carla, I've been to a lot of plays—plays put on by the best professional troupes in the world, like the Royal Shakespeare Company in London— and I must say, you are at *least* as good at acting as those people!"

"Oh, go on," I scoffed, waving my hands. "You're just saying that because you're my friends." This time, however, I knew that wasn't true.

"You're a shoo-in for Emily," Betsy assured me. "No doubt about it."

"How about going over to my house for a celebration after the auditions?" Samantha offered. "A performance like that deserves something really special!"

"Thanks," I said modestly. "But the auditions aren't over. Let's see how the others do."

Samantha glanced up at the stage. "Well, it looks like the only one left is Wendy. And you can just imagine how *her* reading is going to be."

Betsy and Samantha were giggling over the way they were expecting the head cheerleader's performance to go. But I was listening carefully, anxious to see it for myself.

"All set, Wendy?" Ms. Hart was asking.

"Sure, I guess so." She was standing with her arms folded across her chest. One hip was thrust out, and her head was cocked to one side.

In other words, she looked as if she couldn't care less about any of this.

"What grade are you in, Wendy?"

"Seventh."

Then she did something that nearly knocked me off my seat. She snapped her gum.

"Uh, Wendy?" Ms. Hart said, sounding irritated for the first time since the auditions had begun. "Would you please lose the gum?"

"Huh? Oh, sure." Wendy, looking bewildered, reached into her pocket and took out a small piece of paper, then wrapped her gum in it and stuck the whole wad back.

"Where were we?" asked Ms. Hart. "Oh, yes. Do you have any previous acting experience?"

Wendy tossed her long blond hair, then stood up straight and folded her hands behind her back. "Not exactly."

"Not exactly? What does that mean?"

"I've been in school plays and all that, but I've never had a real speaking part. You know, like the lead or anything."

"I see."

Behind me, Betsy and Samantha could barely contain themselves. They were giggling and whispering so much I was surprised they could even hear anything that was going on. But at least they were being pretty quiet about it. As far as I could tell, nobody else could hear them.

I, meanwhile, was watching carefully. Sure, it was obvious that Wendy was acting like a total dork. But I had to admit that she looked pretty good, standing up there on the stage. She was tall and thin, with that long blond hair. . . .

Don't even *think* it, I warned myself.

Still, when Ms. Hart asked her the next question, my heart sunk somewhere down into my stomach, around about where my ice-cream sandwich from lunch was sitting.

"What part are you going to be reading?"

"Emily."

It made perfect sense, of course, and I shouldn't have been the least bit surprised. Still, it suddenly felt as if the air in the auditorium was about six hundred years old.

"That's good," Betsy was saying to Samantha. "Wendy is going to make Carla's performance look even better!"

I held my breath as Wendy began to read. She had chosen a different scene, one in which her character is talking about marrying George Gibbs, something she's not sure she wants to do. That scene had been my second choice. I was glad I hadn't picked it.

I was more nervous during Wendy's reading than I had been during my own. But even in my half-panicked state, I had to admit that I didn't have very much to worry about.

Wendy's reading was terrible.

First of all, she just stood there. I mean, she wasn't using her body at all. True, she was holding the script, and that didn't help things very much. Even so, she didn't use any arm movements, not even any facial expressions.

She didn't *act* like Emily.

As for her voice, it sounded stiff. It sounded . . . well, as if she were reading from a script. And it was very hard to hear her. In fact, I suspected that if the auditorium had been filled with people—coughing, shuffling, just *breathing*—it would have been impossible.

But I had to admit, once again, that she *looked* good.

The section she read wasn't very long. Before we knew it, it was over.

"Thank you, Wendy," Ms. Hart said.

Wendy peered over at her, blinking and looking puzzled. "That's it? You mean I'm done?"

"You're done, and the whole audition is over. That is, unless I missed somebody. . . ."

"Want to try out?" Samantha whispered to Betsy.

"No, thanks. I'll leave the acting to the expert over here."

I just smiled.

"So, Kelly, how did your first day of work go?" my father asked over dinner.

The four of us were sitting around the table Monday evening, stuffing our faces. It was pizza night at the Farrell house, one of those institutions that pops up whenever everyone in the family is either too busy, too tired, or simply not interested enough to cook up a real meal. Tonight's selection was one straight from the top of my list: half pepperoni, half mushroom. Just the thing to celebrate that afternoon's victory at the drama club auditions.

Not that that was what we were talking about at the moment. As usual, it was my sister and her thrilling life that Mom and Dad were most interested in hearing about.

"My first day was great!" Kelly replied. "I really had fun."

"Fun!" My father pretended to be horrified. "Since when is an after-school job supposed to be *fun*?"

Kelly laughed. "Oh, Daddy, it *was* fun. It was great. I met so many new people—"

"How many of them were boys?" I mumbled into my slice of mushroom pizza.

"And I turned out to be really good at it. Mr. Deegan told me I was one of the fastest cashiers he's ever had working for him! I'm pretty good at sales, too. I talked this one girl into buying an outfit she just couldn't make up her mind about.'' Quickly she added, "Of course, she really did look good in it, and it was a very good buy.''

"Terrific,'' Dad said. "Before we know it, we're going to have the president of the Clothes Circuit company living in our house.''

Kelly giggled. "Oh, Daddy. We'll have to see about that. I am brand new at this, don't forget. In fact, Mr. Deegan hung around the store most of the time, since it was my first time and all. Tomorrow afternoon, he's going to leave me alone in the store, along with this other girl who works after school. Her name is Jaimie. But from what I've seen so far, I'm much better at the job than she is.''

"Cashier of the Year,'' I told a lump of cheese.

"And believe it or not, I've already decided how I'm going to spend my first paycheck,'' Kelly went on happily. "This terrific new line of jewelry just came into the store today. They're papier-mâché bracelets and matching earrings in the wildest colors. We've got them in this special display, right next to the cash register. The bracelets are eight dollars, and the earrings are five. So as soon as I've got a little cash in my pocket . . .'' She sighed. "I just can't decide between the hot pink with orange and the lime green with yellow.''

"Nobody ever said being a fashion plate was easy,'' I commented to the last piece of crust I was about to devour.

Which led me to check out just how much pizza

was left. I discovered that the half with the pepperoni was going fast.

"Hey, that last piece of pepperoni pizza has my name on it," I insisted. "Get your mitts off it."

Kelly looked up at me and blinked. It was as if she had totally forgotten that she had a sister.

"How about you, Carla?" she asked. Already she had bypassed that last slice of pepperoni and was instead attacking a slice of the mushroom. "How did your day go?"

"I thought you'd never ask," I replied. "Today was . . . how can I put this? Wonderful, fantastic, marvelous, awesome—"

"My goodness!" my mother exclaimed. "What happened today, Carla?"

"The auditions for the school play, that's what. *Our Town*, remember? Thornton Wilder? One of America's classics? Also one of American theater's great roles. The part of Emily, I mean."

"Is that the part you got?" Kelly asked.

"That's the part I tried out for. I don't know yet—for *sure*, I mean—whether or not I got it. Not *officially*, that is."

From the way my eyes were glowing, I was sure Mom and Dad and Kelly got the point: that the three of them were sitting side by side with the future Emily Webb of Hanover Junior High School's production of *Our Town*.

"Well, congratulations!" My father was beaming. The look on his face, I decided, was at least as rewarding as the sound of the audience's applause was going to be on opening night.

Still, I had to keep things in perspective.

"It's not *completely* definite," I told him. "I'll find out for sure tomorrow, right after school. That's when the results of the auditions are going to be posted."

Kelly reached over and gave my shoulder a squeeze. "I'll be keeping my fingers crossed for you," she said earnestly.

"We all will," my mother said.

I didn't mention that my own fingers were already developing cramps from spending so much time being crossed.

"Goodness, what successful daughters I have!" my father exclaimed. "I'm so proud I could . . . I could finish off the rest of this pizza!"

"You'd better not," I insisted. "I'm celebrating tonight, and that means the sky's the limit. At least, when it comes to eating pizza." I pretended not to notice the look my parents exchanged. Besides, I was in such a good mood that I wasn't about to let anything get me down. I was flying high. Even Kelly's success wasn't bothering me.

Not tonight, when it seemed as if everything in the whole world was simply perfect.

# chapter
## five

The next morning, I woke up with butterflies in my stomach. They were happy butterflies, though. Excited butterflies. Butterflies that couldn't stop thinking about the fact that this was the day that the results of the *Our Town* auditions were going to be posted.

I decided to treat my butterflies to a special breakfast: a stack of toaster waffles dripping with maple syrup and butter.

"Today's the day," Betsy greeted me as I strolled into English class an hour later. "What time are they posting the casting list?"

"Not until after school," I replied. I made a face to demonstrate just how far away that sounded. "Right after the last bell."

"Oh, Carla," Samantha cried, "how are you ever going to make it through the whole day?"

I sank into my chair. "I have a feeling that I'm going to spend a lot of time looking at the clock."

That turned out to be an understatement. The day seemed to crawl along, the longest Tuesday since the

Ice Age. Carefully I monitored its snail-paced progress, glancing at my wristwatch at least every five minutes. Two of my teachers commented on my sudden obsession with the time. But I couldn't help it.

I was beginning to think that three o'clock would never, ever come. But then, finally, the last bell rang. I shot out of my seat and dashed toward the auditorium. It was on the bulletin board right outside that the results of the audition were going to be posted.

Once I rounded the corner and the bulletin board was in sight, I tried to calm down. Instead of doing the kind of running-skipping kind of motion that had gotten me there, I slowed down to a walk. I wanted to at least *appear* casual, even if my heart was beating about a jillion times a second.

I sauntered over. Quickly I skimmed the notices that were posted there: an announcement about the Halloween Dance committee, a reminder that basketball tryouts were being held that Friday, a notice about a bake sale that was coming up.

Then I spotted it. *"Our Town,"* it said on top, the letters bold and black. Listed below, on the left, were the familiar names of all the characters, in the order that they appeared on the stage. The Stage Manager was way at the top. I wasn't at all surprised to see that Andrew Morris had gotten that role.

But it was hardly my main interest. I quickly skimmed the list—Dr. Gibbs, Mrs. Gibbs, Rebecca Gibbs . . . and then there it was. Emily Webb.

The name written to the right of it was Wendy Lipton.

"No!" I cried aloud. "It can't be!"

My eyes were glued to that group of four words. Emily Webb . . . Wendy Lipton. That was *my* part. Mine! And it had gone to the wrong person!

"How did you do?" I suddenly heard someone say, not far behind me.

"Did you get the part?" another voice asked.

Samantha and Betsy were beside me, clutching their schoolbooks to their chests, peering at the same sheet of paper I was staring at.

"Where's Carla's name?" Betsy was saying.

"Did you make it? Are you Emily?" Samantha asked.

"Here's your name, Carla," Betsy cried. Then, sounding puzzled, she added, "But it looks like you got the part of Mrs. Webb."

"Mrs. Webb!" I cried. "Where? Where does it say that?"

Betsy pointed to the sheet.

"Oh, no!" I had this sudden, overwhelming urge to burst into tears. "Not Mrs. Webb!"

I swallowed hard. "She's old. She's frumpy. She's a character part. She's . . . she's . . ."

I could barely go on. Only reminding myself that these two girls were my best friends in the world made it possible. Even then, my voice came out as a sob.

"Mrs. Webb is Emily Webb's *mother*!"

"Oh, Carla," Samantha cooed.

I could tell she was about to say something sympathetic, or maybe something hopeful. But she never got a chance. All of a sudden a cyclone happened by—a cyclone in the form of Wendy Lipton and her best friend and reliable sidekick, Kicky.

"Oh, *there* it is," Kicky cried. "The casting list is over on that bulletin board."

She practically knocked into us before she said, "Oh, hello, Carla. I didn't even notice you."

She glanced at the list. Then, wearing a smug smile, she said in this really loud voice, "Gee, Wendy, it looks like you got the prime role. You're going to play Emily Webb."

Wendy just tossed her head. "Terrific. Now we'd better hurry if we're going to be on time for cheerleading practice. You know I always like to fix my makeup right before."

Betsy and Samantha and I were silent for a long time after Wendy and Kicky had left. Finally, in a strained kind of voice, Betsy said, "Maybe there's been a mistake."

I shook my head. "No, Betsy. No mistake."

"Maybe it's not too late for Ms. Hart to change her mind," Samantha offered next, in that same weak, hopeful voice.

Biting my lip, I said, "We all know that's not the case. Look, maybe it's not so terrible. I still get to be in the play. And Mrs. Webb is a pretty good role. You know, when you come right down to it, it's really much more difficult to play a character part. This will be much more of a challenge for me. I'll get to act like somebody much older than I am, and . . . and wear makeup and clothes that'll make me look like her. . . ." I couldn't go on. Being a good sport was one thing. Lying through my teeth was something else entirely.

"Hey, I know," Samantha said brightly. "How about coming over to my house? I just got some great new tapes. We could hang out there for a while."

"No, thanks," I said, before Betsy had a chance to jump on the bandwagon. "If you don't mind, I think I'd rather be alone for a while."

Betsy and Samantha looked at each other, the expressions on their faces making it clear that they were both worried about me.

But I forced a smile. "Look, you guys. I'll survive. Really I will. I just . . . I think I'll take a walk or something, okay?"

Up until that point, I had figured that, no matter what, I'd always want to be surrounded by the other members of the Bubble Gum Gang. Good times, bad times, any kind of times. But at that moment, for the first time since I'd become friends with Betsy and Samantha, I was feeling so low that all I wanted was to be by myself.

In fact, the only thing in the world that I was looking forward to was finding a quiet corner, curling up in it, and having a good cry.

I did end up taking a walk—but not the kind Betsy and Samantha thought I was going to take. Rather than going outside to bask in the beauty of the sun and the trees on a crisp early autumn day, my stroll took me down the corridor and up the stairs of the school building. I ended up right outside Ms. Hart's classroom, where she taught eighth- and ninth-grade English.

I wasn't certain what I was going to say. All I knew was, given the way I felt, I had to say *something*. If I didn't, I was going to burst into two. Or at least burst into tears. I still hadn't entirely ruled out that possibility.

What I wanted to tell her, of course, was how much getting the part of Emily meant to me. How good I knew I could be in the role. And—if I could find a way to say it in a reasonably nice, polite way— how *bad* Wendy Lipton was bound to be in it.

As I neared her classroom, however, I could hear voices coming from inside. As I had been hoping, she was in there, all right, but she wasn't alone. I decided to wait. I leaned against the wall, just outside the open door.

I didn't mean to eavesdrop; really I didn't. All I wanted was to get close enough to hear when the conversation ended so I'd know it was time for me to put my thoughts together and make my grand entrance.

If I had realized I was going to overhear—and if I had any idea *what* it was I was going to overhear—I never in a million years would have stood so close.

"Of *course* it's going to be difficult, getting Wendy Lipton to come across in a favorable light," Ms. Hart was saying. "But I'll manage somehow. I'll have to. I still believe she was the best person for the role of Emily."

"Wasn't there anyone else who could have played that part?"

I recognized that second voice right away. It belonged to Mr. Homer, my English teacher.

"You know as well as I do that it's a very important role," Ms. Hart replied. "And if the play is going to work, it's vital that the girl who plays Emily be the prettiest girl in the production."

There was a long pause.

"Tell me, did Carla Farrell try out for the play, by any chance?"

"Yes, she did. And she did an excellent job. I assigned her the part of Mrs. Webb. I have a feeling she's going to steal the show."

"I figured she'd audition, and that she'd do a good job. She mentioned something in class about having been in a play over the summer. In fact, I wonder . . . wouldn't she have done a better job at playing Emily?"

I was holding my breath. There it was, the exact same question I had been dying to ask. Mr. Homer was doing it for me. I felt like rushing in there and throwing my arms around him in gratitude. Instead, I leaned just a little bit closer so I could hear more clearly.

When I heard Ms. Hart's response, it was all I could do to keep from gasping.

"You can't be serious."

"Why not?" Mr. Homer demanded. "You told me yourself Carla did a fine job at the audition. You just said you expected her to steal the show."

"Yes . . . in a *character* part. But let's face it. For all her acting talent, Carla Farrell does not exactly *look* the part of a star."

There it was. She said it straight out. And even though I knew in my heart that she was right, hearing someone say it didn't do much to make me feel any better. I never heard the end of the conversation. Instead, I took off. All I wanted was to get home, to my own house, to my own room, where I could close the door and shut out the entire world.

Finally, it was getting to be time for that good cry.


After I had gotten that out of the way—lying on my bed, working through half a box of tissues, crying and sobbing and sniffling until my eyes hurt and my nose was as red as Rudolph's—I decided to try looking at things with a different perspective. I came up with sort of a brainstorm: making a list of both the good things and the bad things about this situation.

There was nobody else home, which was fine with me. Kelly was at the mall—knocking 'em dead over at Clothes Circuit, no doubt, with her breathtaking skill at the cash register. My dad was at work, and my mom was out doing errands. So with the entire house to myself, I ventured out of the safety of my bedroom and sat down at the dining room table, ready to tackle my newfound project head-on.

I opened one of my school notebooks to a clean page. Drawing a long, straight line, I divided it up into two columns. At the top of one, I wrote "Pro's." At the top of the other, I wrote "Con's." I was all set.

I stared at the page for a long time. Finally, under the "Pro's" column, I wrote, 1) I get to be in the play. 2) I get to play a major role. 3) I get to try a character part.

There. That looked pretty good. Next I headed over to the "Con's." I stared and stared, thinking and thinking, and then, with deep, bold strokes of my pen I wrote, "I GOT CHEATED OUT OF *MY* PART!"

So much for that idea.

I was still disappointed. Worse than that, I was really, really angry. How *dare* Ms. Hart give my part to someone else, mainly because she happened to be as skinny as a department store mannequin, while I was somewhat more . . . round?

I decided to bury my bad mood in a nice big hunk of chocolate cake. Sure, it was getting close to dinner time, but that had never stopped me before. I knew there was some leftover cake in the refrigerator; I had checked that out first thing after arriving home. It was right behind the big bowl of salad that my mother always kept there, mostly for Kelly but also for herself.

I had just sat down at the kitchen table with a glass of milk and the cake when I heard a commotion at the front door. Kelly came storming in, yelling, "Anybody home?" Her voice sounded kind of weird, I thought.

"Kelly?" I said, standing up and walking out to the front hallway. "Are you okay?"

"Where's Mom?" she demanded. She was standing there staring at me, with this really odd look on her face. "Is she here?"

"No. I'm the only one who's here. Dad's at work, Mom's out—"

"Good," she said, more to herself than to me.

"Kelly," I asked, puzzled, "is there something wrong?"

All of a sudden she burst out crying. There she was, my perfect sister with the perfect life, standing in front of me with tears cascading down her face like Niagara Falls. Her makeup was melting all over the place.

"What is it?" I demanded. "What happened?"

"Oh, Carla!" she sobbed. "This has been the worst day of my entire life."

"Join the club," I muttered. "What happened?"

I could only imagine. She probably broke a nail, or scuffed up her new shoes, or maybe some stupendous boy she had had her eye on asked somebody else out. . . . Given the way my thoughts were going, I was totally unprepared for what was coming.

"Oh, Carla! You won't believe this." Kelly's eyes were brimming with a brand new tidal wave of tears. "Mr. Deegan accused me of *stealing*!"

# chapter
## six

"I *didn't* steal that bracelet off the counter," Kelly
sobbed, grabbing at the seventeenth tissue she had
used since she plopped down cross-legged on my
bed.

It occurred to me that the way tissues were going
in my house that day, maybe it was time to start
buying them by the case. But that was the least of
my concerns as Kelly and I sat holed up in my bedroom. Even though nobody else was home, we had
locked the door. After all, about every two minutes,
Kelly would look at me with this terrible panicked
expression on her face and plead, "*Please*, Carla!
Don't tell Mom and Dad about this!"

"I believe you, Kelly," I insisted. "You don't have
to try to convince me. I mean, I *know* you. I know
you'd never steal."

Kelly made a loud sniffling sound. She reached for
tissue number eighteen. Then, biting her lip, she
said, "Well, it certainly wasn't easy convincing Mr.
Deegan of that."

"But you did manage to make him believe that you

weren't the one who took the papier-mâché bracelet that was missing, right?''

Kelly nodded, blowing her nose at the same time.

"Tell me about it again," I urged. "Go back to the very beginning."

It took a few seconds for my sister to pull herself together. In the meantime, I put my arm around her shoulders, trying to comfort her. It felt kind of weird, since 99 percent of the time, things went the other way around.

"Okay," Kelly said, taking a few deep breaths. "This is what happened. I went to work at three o'clock, just like I was supposed to. I spent the whole afternoon at the cash register or helping customers.

"Boy, was it busy! Clothes Circuit is running a big grand-opening sale, and everything in the Neon Niche was half price. The place was packed. Anyway, there I was, working my tail off, trying to ring up sales and at the same time help customers who were looking for a particular size or who insisted that I go check in back to see if we had any more stock."

"It sounds like you were totally frazzled," I said sympathetically. "I mean, you never even would have noticed if somebody reached over and helped herself to one of those bracelets."

"That's right. I can't be everywhere at the same time. I *am* only one person. Besides, I was totally wrapped up in trying to do everything right: working the cash register, helping the customers. . . . That *is* what Mr. Deegan pays me for, after all."

I gave her shoulders a little squeeze. "Go on. What happened next?"

"Well, around five-thirty, right before I was suppose to leave, Mr. Deegan came by. He wanted to know how the sale was going. He was particularly interested in the jewelry, because it was a new line and all. He checked the display and said, 'Gee, I see you already sold three of the bracelets.' And I said, 'Actually, I've been so busy that I haven't been keeping track.' He started checking through the receipts for the afternoon, wanting to see for himself what was selling and what wasn't, and the next thing I knew, he told me there were only receipts for *two* bracelets.''

Kelly stopped to get her bearings. I had a sneaking suspicion that tissue number nineteen wasn't long for this world. "That was when he started getting really upset. He kept asking me what happened to the third bracelet, and I kept saying I didn't know. Finally he begin to imply that I had taken it. I wanted to prove he was wrong, so I emptied my pockets right in front of him. I even went to the back of the store and got my pocketbook to show him I didn't have the bracelet!''

Kelly made a loud hiccupping sound. All that crying was starting to catch up with her. "Anyway, by that point I had burst into tears. Jaimie came over to see what was going on, and she showed him her purse and her pockets to prove she hadn't taken the bracelet. . . . Oh, Carla! It was such a mess. What a scene. It was like something out of a movie!''

"But you finally convinced him that you were innocent?''

Kelly nodded. "He *had* to believe me. He could

see for himself that I didn't have the missing bracelet."

"But that doesn't mean the real culprit has been
caught," I said. "Hmmm. Let's see now. How about
the people who were shopping? Was there anybody
in the store this afternoon who looked suspicious?
Somebody who . . . oh, I don't know, hung around
for a really long time but didn't buy anything? Or
. . . or . . ."

"Not that I noticed," Kelly replied. She looked
kind of confused by all this.

"Wait. Let's go back to the other girl who works
in the store. This Jaimie. Kelly, are you sure she
wasn't the one who took the bracelet?"

She shook her head. "Practically the entire afternoon, she was at the other cash register, the one in
the back of the store.

"Maybe so . . . but are you sure she didn't come
over to the counter where the bracelets were on display at all? Not even once?"

I was beginning to feel like one of the detectives
I was always seeing on TV, giving somebody the
third degree. But the truth was that I really wanted
to know. There was a real mystery here, one that my
sister was caught up in, and I was determined to get
to the bottom of it. Or at least to find out as much
as I could.

Kelly shook her head. "No, I didn't see Jaimie
near the bracelets. But that doesn't mean really mean
anything," she added quickly. "I mean, I did end
up making quite a few trips out back to the stock
room. And I was tied up with customers a lot of the

time." She sighed tiredly. "You wouldn't believe how demanding some people can be."

"Ahah! So for all we know, it *could* have been Jaimie who snuck over to the counter up near your register and helped herself to the bracelet."

Kelly's eyes grew big and round. "Oh, Carla! I would never want to blame Jaimie! She's so nice! She's been so helpful, right from the start. After all, I was new and she had worked at another store before this—"

"Kelly," I said evenly, "I'm not accusing Jaimie of anything. I'm just trying to figure out what could have happened. And that's one way that it could have happened, right?"

"Well . . . I suppose so."

"Okay. So far we have two possible suspects: Jaimie, and one of the shoppers."

"I—I guess so."

My sister looked totally miserable. In fact, she looked the way I had been feeling all afternoon. Now, of course, I was too wrapped up in this new development to be thinking about myself and my problems. In fact, that could have been one reason why I was taking such an interest in Kelly's catastrophe.

"Okay. So the picture is beginning to come into focus." I kind of wished I had one of those little spiral notebooks so I could whip it out of my pocket and jot down notes. "Bracelet, Jaimie, shopper . . . Am I missing anything?"

Kelly looked at me with these big, sad, puppy dog eyes.

"Well, at one point, when the store was at its busiest, a few of my friends came in to say hello."

I frowned. "How well do you know these kids?"

"Oh, Carla! I'm not going to start wondering if any of them stole that bracelet! They're my *friends*!"

"I know," I said calmly. "But the fact remains that you were accused of stealing something you didn't take. Sure, you finally convinced Mr. Deegan that you were innocent. But even so, we can't just sit by, Kelly. We have to explore every possibility, no matter how farfetched it might sound!"

Kelly, sitting up once again, covered her face with her hands. "Oh, Carla, let's just let it go, okay? I don't even want to talk about it anymore."

She let out a long, exhausted sigh. "Just do me a favor. Don't say a word to Mom and Dad, okay? I mean, the whole incident is over, as far as I'm concerned."

"But Kelly, don't you think they should know about this? I mean, Mr. Deegan *did* accuse you. Maybe he still has some suspicions about you. Who knows? This could even snowball into something worse."

Kelly looked at me, blinking. "Look, Carla, I know you mean well. But I really don't want to bring Mom and Dad into the picture. I don't even know if I'm going to tell them. Working at the mall, getting my first real job . . . That was all really important to me, you know? Here I wanted to show Mom and Dad that I could do it. I wanted so badly to act grown-up. And now . . . and now *this*."

I opened my mouth to offer still another argument

for going to Mom and Dad. But one more look at my sister told me it was time for me to butt out.

Poor Kelly. Here I had always thought my big sister—my pretty, popular, *thin* big sister—had the ideal life. Things always seemed to go exactly the way she wanted. She had everything: friends, boyfriends, good looks, even the kind of after-school job she had always wanted.

And now, much to my amazement, I was finding that things weren't so easy for her, either. Even she could have bad experiences, terrible, upsetting ones like what had happened to her today.

It was kind of strange, discovering that for the first time in my life, I actually felt sorry for Kelly.

"Oh, no! She was actually accused of stealing a bracelet?" Betsy breathed.

"And she had to show her boss it wasn't in her purse before he'd believe she was innocent?" Samantha sounded just as amazed. "Oh, Carla, your poor sister!"

It was just before first-period English class, the very next day. While Kelly had asked me not to tell my parents about the terrible scene at Clothes Circuit, that certainly didn't mean I couldn't confide in my two best friends in the entire world. After all, if I couldn't trust the other members of the Bubble Gum Gang, who *could* I trust?

And just as I had expected, both Samantha and Betsy were sympathetic.

"Well, at least she managed to convince Mr. Deegan that she was innocent," I replied, keeping my voice low. "But there's one thing that hasn't been cleared up, and that's the question of who really *did* take the bracelet."

We still had a good two minutes before the bell was going to ring. Mr. Homer was at the front of the room, busily trying to get the blackboards perfectly clean. They were already clean, as far as I could tell, but then again, he's really compulsive about some things.

"Well, Carla," Betsy said then, "what are *you* going to do?"

"What?"

"You are her sister, right? And there has been a terrible injustice committed."

Betsy was speaking in this very matter-of-fact tone, like, of course I know what I'm talking about.

"I mean, poor Kelly is being accused of a crime she didn't commit. Not only that, but the store where she works has been *robbed*. You're certainly not going to just stand there, are you?"

My mouth had dropped open so far that my lower jaw was somewhere down around my collar.

"Me?" I squawked. "What on earth could *I* do?"

It was Samantha who answered that question. "It wouldn't be just you, of course."

"Oh, no?" I grumbled. "And who's going to help me, Wonder Woman?"

"The next best thing." Betsy was beaming. "The Bubble Gum Gang, of course!"

"That's right," Samantha agreed. "After all, why did we form the Bubble Gum Gang in the first place if not to solve mysteries?"

Betsy nodded. "Especially if the mystery in question involves someone whom one of us actually knows."

"You mean . . . you mean you two would help me find out what happened to the disappearing bracelet?"

It's not that I'm hard of hearing or anything. I just couldn't quite grasp the idea that these two people— these two wonderful, darling, sweet people—were actually going to help out here. And they weren't only helping me. Or Kelly—whom, I might mention, they hardly even knew. No, it went beyond that. We were talking about serving the greater cause of justice: helping Mr. Deegan find out who was responsible for making off with his merchandise.

"Are you kidding?" Samantha said. "I don't know about you, but ever since we formed the Bubble Gum Gang, I've been dying to get involved in a case. Some mystery, or some puzzle . . ."

"Hopefully, one that doesn't involve ghosts," Betsy added with a giggle, referring to the haunted house escapade that had first brought us all together.

"I don't think we're dealing with ghosts here," I said seriously. "Although that would certainly be a convenient way of explaining the mystery of the disappearing bracelet."

"No, no ghosts this time, but you've made a good point," Samantha said. "And that is that I don't think we're going to figure out this mystery quite as easily as the last one."

"But we do have a couple of clues," Betsy remarked. "One is that we know there's something going on. Another is that it's going on at Clothes Circuit.''

"Hmmm." I scratched my head monkey-style as I thought, just like people are always doing in cartoons. "Maybe we should head over to the mall and check things out. You know, take a look around, poke our noses in a few corners, ask a few questions. . . ."

"That sounds like a good idea," Samantha said.

"Wait a minute. I have an even better idea."

All of a sudden Betsy had this strange look in her eyes. They were kind of glowing, as if she were getting really, really excited.

"In fact, you might even say I've had a real brainstorm."

She leaned forward and whispered her idea to us. I had to admit, it was a good one. Ingenious, in fact. I'd even go so far as to say that it qualified as a *major* brainstorm.

Samantha agreed. "Of *course*!" she cried. "That's exactly what we should do, Betsy. Now why on earth didn't I think of that?"

"Because you and I aren't quite as advanced as old Betsy here in the brain power department," I said admiringly.

"Give me a break!" Betsy cried, her cheeks turning bright red. But then she laughed. "Sometimes it pays off to be an egghead."

At the moment, instead of looking embarrassed about the fact that she was probably the smartest girl in the entire school—including eighth and ninth graders, as well as our own grade level—she was looking very satisfied.

"Okay, we need a plan," she went on. "Carla, when is the next time your sister works at Clothes Circuit?"

"Let me see," I said, trying to remember. "Her schedule during the week is Mondays, Tuesdays, and Thursdays, right after school."

"And today is Wednesday," Betsy said, nodding. "Good. That gives us a day to work out all the details. Uh oh, I just thought of something. Carla, do you have a rehearsal after school tomorrow?"

The play. I had been so wrapped up in Kelly's catastrophe that I had forgotten all about it. "Nope. I'll be free to play the role of private investigator then. There's a rehearsal today after school, but tomorrow is reserved for the kids who have the biggest parts."

Like Andrew Morris, who was playing the Stage Manager. And, well, like Wendy Lipton, who of course was playing Emily Webb.

I waited, expecting to feel a tug of sorrow, or jealousy, or *something*. Instead, I found myself thinking about how insignificant it seemed, not getting the part in the school play that I wanted. Compared to what my sister had been put through, being assigned the part of Emily Webb's mother instead of Emily Webb didn't seem any more important than . . . than which sweater I had decided to wear to school that day.

I *would* care again, I knew. It would matter later on that same day, when our first rehearsal got going and I had to confront the sight of Wendy Lipton up there on stage, bumbling through what should have been my part.

But at the moment, I was thinking about other things. How terrible it must have felt to be in Kelly's shoes the day before. How really, really wonderful it would be if the Bubble Gum Gang could get to the bottom of this intriguing little mystery.

And how really, really, *really* glad I was that I had good friends like Betsy Crane and Samantha Langtree.

# chapter
## seven

As the day went on, I found myself thinking about Kelly less and less . . . and the rehearsal scheduled for after school that day more and more. In fact, it wasn't long before I couldn't concentrate on anything else. I kept thinking about the summer before, remembering how much I had loved rehearsals. And here I was, about to do it all over again. I kept picturing myself after the last bell, dashing to my locker, racing to the auditorium, knowing I had someplace important to go.

Unfortunately, it didn't take me long to find out that being in this play was not going to be exactly the same as being in the *other* play.

"All right, boys and girls." Ms. Hart clapped her hands crisply, meanwhile striding up to the front of the auditorium. She was certainly turning out to have one of those take-charge personalities. "Please quiet down now."

Those of us who were in the play were sitting in the first few rows of the auditorium, spread out all over the place instead of scrunching together. I have to admit, I was feeling pretty excited at this point. At last things were getting underway. And I, meanwhile, was thrilled simply to be part of it. My love of acting, my passion for being part of the world of theater, was—at the risk of sounding corny—being reawakened. My heart was pounding away, and I felt as if I could run ten miles, or at least make it around the block.

"Today, I'd like to run through the first act of the play," Ms. Hart said once the rustling of scripts and the whispering and the shuffling of feet had quieted down. "All the characters who appear in Act One, please get up on stage. We'll start reading through, starting on page one. That means we'll begin with the Stage Manager, the first one to speak. Andrew Morris, where are you? Where is my Stage Manager?"

Andrew was already bounding up to the stage, looking very serious.

"Now, where are all my other Act One people? I want you up on stage as well. Dr. Gibbs? Joe Crowell, Jr.? Professor Willard? Mrs. Webb?"

Actually, just about everybody who was in the play appeared in the first act. So it was pretty crowded as we all filed up to the stage. First Ms. Hart showed us where each one of us was supposed to be standing while different parts of the dialogue were being spoken. That's called blocking. Then she shooed all of us backstage—all of us, that is, except Andrew.

Since he played the part of the Stage Manager, he was the one who got the ball rolling. And then it was time to start. Andrew began reading from the script, starting with a really long monologue all about the town where the play is set, Grover's Corners. As I've already said, the play is about finding joy in the simplicity of small-town life, appreciating the people we love and the day-to-day events that make up our lives. Most people, the playwright felt, just zoom right through it without taking the time to notice how wonderful it all is.

Andrew was doing a great job, just like I knew he would. He was little bit stiff at first, but it didn't take him long to get into it. He was good at putting his whole body into his acting, moving around the stage as he pointed out different things in the town by way of introducing it to the audience: Mrs. Gibbs' garden, the public school, the grocery store, that kind of thing.

I suppose I should also mention that one of the things about the play is that there's no scenery to speak of. I think that's because Thornton Wilder, who wrote the play, figured that it wasn't fancy scenery that counted in plays; it was what was going on between the characters. Anyway, whether he was right or not, it sure made it easy to put that play on. Even though we were doing our initial reading on a stage that was practically bare, it looked pretty much the way it was going to look on opening night.

So there was Andrew, doing this crackerjack job. From off-stage, behind the curtain, where I was standing, I could see that Ms. Hart was pleased. She was sitting in the front row, the script in her lap, watching closely and occasionally calling out directions, like ''A little louder, Stage Manager!'' and ''You're too far back. Move up a little!''

Then, it was time for a few more of us to go onto the stage. Paul Green, who was playing Dr. Gibbs, needed a good shove to get him out there. I guess he was so busy listening to Andrew's terrific monologue that he forgot that he was a part of the play, too.

I was right behind him. As Mrs. Webb, I was supposed to wander out onto the stage, tying on my apron. I guess one more thing I should mention that in addition to having no real scenery, this play doesn't have any real props, either. The actors are supposed to *pretend* they're there. To pantomime.

That, fortunately, happens to be one of the things I'm especially good at. So there I was was, walking onto the stage, pretending I was putting on this invisible apron. And then, following the directions in the script, I went through the motions of pretending to light an old-fashioned wood stove.

The weird thing is, I could practically *see* that stove. It was big and dark and heavy, made out of wrought iron. I could feel the invisible wood as I fed it into the invisible fire, just the way I could feel the nonexistent fabric of the ties as I put on my apron.

That's the great thing about acting. Up there on stage, absolutely *anything* can happen.

So I was keeping busy up there, still messing around with my imaginary stove as some of the other characters read their lines. The lines in the script consisted of the kind of small talk that people make every day of their lives, talking about the weather and the health of their friends and that kind of stuff.

Then it was my turn to speak. My opening lines consisted of calling to my daughter, Emily, telling her to wake up and start getting ready for school. Not exactly high drama, but I did my best. Besides, simply having the chance to say anything at all was a kick.

Just as I expected, I was finding the whole thing enthralling. How exciting it was, watching what, up until that point, had simply been words on a page suddenly coming to life! I mean, I know that sounds weird, but that's exactly what was happening. It really *was* coming to life. The printed page was becoming the actual words that real people were speaking.

Well, *almost* real people. They were actually kids at my school, pretending to be those particular people. But that didn't matter. All that mattered was that it was thrilling, exhilirating, inspiring. . . .

And then, Wendy Lipton came sashaying onto the stage.

It was time for the character of Emily to make her entrance. But instead of looking like a bright, cheerful, wholesome teenaged girl right after the turn of the century, rushing down to breakfast with her little brother, she was acting as if she were strolling through a shopping mall.

And as if that wasn't bad enough, she read off her first line in this really whiny, singsong voice.

To me, it sounded like fingernails screeching on a chalk board.

All of a sudden, I was finding it hard to stay in character. Just having her up there on stage was totally ruining my concentration. But I did my best to muddle through.

"Wendy Lipton is only *one* of the people in the play," I told myself. "Think about all the others. Try thinking about Andrew, and what a terrific job he's doing as Stage Manager."

I managed to hang on. That is, until we started getting close to the end of Act One and it was time for Mrs. Webb—that's me—and Emily to have a conversation.

The other characters had moved away and the spotlight was on Wendy and me. It's one of those classic mother-daughter moments. It's supposed to be sweet and nice and all that, with dear little Emily asking me, her mom, whether or not she's pretty.

I gave my line, and then, in response, Wendy was supposed to say "I don't know," sounding really distracted, as if she wasn't really listening.

Instead, I suddenly heard, "*I-I-I* don't know."

I looked up from the imaginary string beans I was supposed to be preparing during this tender moment and saw Wendy Lipton standing there with her hands on her hips, dressed in these pink and white running shoes and an outfit off the cover of *Sassy* magazine, looking like she was getting ready to do the team cheer.

I gritted my teeth. This was turning out to be a lot harder than I had ever dreamed.

I said my next line through those same clenched teeth.

"Whoa, whoa!" cried a voice from the audience. "Okay. Let's stop a minute."

Everybody looked up, surprised. Ms. Hart was hurrying toward the stage.

"Okay, everybody, let's stop a minute. So far, so good. Things have been going fine. It is only a first reading, after all." She forced a smile.

I'm sure some of the kids actually believed what she was saying.

But then she turned to me.

"Uh, Carla, I do believe that Mrs. Webb is, uh, rather *fond* of Emily. She is her daughter, after all."

"I don't always get along with *my* mother," one of the other girls joked.

I was grateful for the girl's attempt at changing the mood. Unfortunately it didn't help much, even though a few of the kids laughed.

What about Wendy? I was tempted to say. She's not exactly a shoo-in for an Oscar. But I didn't. I couldn't.

"Carla," Ms. Hart said gently, "get in character, all right? Let's *all* try our hardest," she finished in this forced, hearty voice. Then she went back to the front row.

I swallowed hard and tried to get ready to con-

tinue. According to the script, the conversation between the two of us went on.

I tried; I really did. I *wanted* to be Mrs. Webb. I
*wanted* to talk to Wendy Lipton as if she were my
daughter, someone I loved dearly. But every time I
looked up and saw her—this girl who wasn't Emily
Webb at all, but Wendy Lipton, the kind of girl who
had always had everything so easy and wasn't even
tuned-in enough to appreciate it—I found it impossible.

And so once again, instead of sounding loving as
I half scolded my dear, sweet daughter for doubting
her prettiness, the way my lines came out made me
sound like a jail warden yelling at one of the in-
mates. I sounded awful, even to me.

Emily had just started to deliver her line when I
heard Ms. Hart again.

"Hold on, everybody." She was back at the edge
of the stage. "Look, I know this is the very first
run-through, and that's always very difficult for everybody. But, uh, let's *all* try to put as much of ourselves into this as we can, all right?"

She was trying to make it sound as if she were
talking to everybody in the cast. But I knew better.
I knew who the bad apple was in this barrel. And
as bizarre as it sounds, I didn't really care.

"Carla, do you have a minute?"

After that rehearsal, the last person in the world I
felt like talking to was Ms. Hart. Yet there she was,
a couple of minutes after it had ended, sort of half

running down the hall toward me as I turned the combination of my locker.

"I guess so." I was glad the metal door opened just then. That way, I could hide my face behind it. "Let me just get the stuff I need out of here," I mumbled. Then, with my arms full of textbooks and notebooks, I turned to face her. "What is it, Ms. Hart?"

From the look on her face, I knew we weren't going to be discussing the weather.

"Carla, why don't we step into one of the classrooms? That way we can have a little more privacy."

It wasn't hard to find an empty classroom, since school had been over for more than an hour. We popped into the closest one. It was a science room, lined with those shiny black desks that had silver spigots sticking out of them.

I deposited all my junk on a chair, sat down on the edge of a desk, and looked at Ms. Hart expectantly.

"Carla," she said, "there's something I want to ask you."

She was having trouble looking me in the eye. I wasn't surprised. I already knew where all this was leading, more or less.

"I don't want to beat around the bush, so I'll just come right out and ask you. Are you *sure* you want to be part of the Drama Club and the *Our Town* production?"

Even though I had been expecting something like

this, my mouth dropped open. "Of *course* I do!" I cried. Goodness, what a question!

"Let me explain," she went on quickly. "I can see that you're good. Your reading at the audition the other day was excellent. You have a real talent, Carla, one that is rare. I'd like to see you develop it. Only . . ."

"Yes?" I asked. I was sincerely interested.

"Only a large part of developing a talent, or any kind of interest, is attitude. You know, the way you really, really feel about what you're doing. Deep down inside."

"But I love acting!" I exclaimed. "When I'm up on the stage, playing a part, I feel as if I'm . . . I'm more alive than at any other time!"

Despite the seriousness of the moment, Ms. Hart smiled. "I can see that you're sincere, Carla. It's obvious that you really do love being part of all this." Her smile vanished as quickly as it had come. "But that only makes me more confused."

"Confused?" I repeated. "About what?"

She paused for a few seconds before going on. "About the way you were behaving today."

All of a sudden *I* was having a hard looking *her* in the eye. "I, uh, I'm sorry about that. I know I wasn't concentrating. I have kind of a lot of things on my mind, and, uh . . ."

"Carla, the stage is no place for acting out your real-life problems." Ms. Hart was speaking in this really kind voice. And the kinder she sounded, the worse I felt.

"I know. I'll do much better next time. I promise!"

Just then, Ms. Hart really surprised me. She reached over and took my hand. "Carla, I know you wanted the part of Emily. I know how disappointed you must be."

I was about to protest, to tell her she was all wrong. Instead, I simply nodded.

"But if you're really interested in theater, there's one very basic thing you'd better learn early on."

"What's that?"

"On the stage, appearance is everything."

I knew I was turning red. I looked down and started playing with the spigot.

"Besides," Ms. Hart went on brightly, "Mrs. Webb is an excellent part. Someone like you, someone with a lot of zip, can really make a part like that come alive. I'm sure you know that it's harder to play a character like Mrs. Webb, one who has depth, than it is to play an innocent young girl like Emily. All Emily has to do is—well, stand there and look pretty and recite her lines. That role is not demanding at all."

"Is that why you gave it to Wendy Lipton?"

I couldn't help it. I just blurted out the words before I had even had a chance to think about them.

Ms. Hart looked startled. She paused, then said, "I think Wendy will do a fine job of playing Emily." She paused before adding, "And Carla?"

"Yes?"

"I think you're going to make a terrific Mrs. Webb." She was wearing a big smile. "In fact, I wouldn't be surprised if you ended up giving one of the best performances this town has ever seen.''

I knew she was trying to make me feel better. And I knew she was only doing what she thought was best, not only for the play but for me. And part of me, a part way down inside, even knew she was right. Why, then, did her little ''pep talk'' only make me feel worse?

# chapter
## eight

"I bet I know who took the bracelet," Betsy announced on Thursday afternoon.

It was right after school, and she and Samantha and I had just taken a seat at the back of the bus headed for the Hanover Mall. We were all filled with a special sense of excitement. After all, we were on a secret mission. This, I was discovering, was much more fun than going to a mall to do something as ordinary as *shop*.

And now, this earth-shattering announcement.

"Really?" I gasped. "Who?"

"Somebody who's out to frame Kelly, that's who."

I looked at her with surprise. "Betsy, who on earth would want to make my sister look like a thief? And, for goodness sake, *why*?"

Betsy shrugged. "I didn't say I had figured out all the details yet. At this stage it's still just a hunch."

"Well, I have a hunch of my own," Samantha said.

I looked over at her and sighed. "Okay, Sam. What's *your* hunch?"

"I think Mr. Deegan stole the bracelet himself!"

"Mr. Deegan! Why on earth would he do that?"

The expression on her face clouded over. "Just like Betsy said, it's still in the hunch stage."

I just had to reach over and give them both a hug.

"Boy, you two are terrific. I really appreciate your doing this. I mean, giving up your free time after school to go to the mall with me like this, just so you can help me get to the bottom of this mystery. . . ." I laughed. "I just hope we three sleuths can manage to come up with something more than hunches!"

"Sure we will," Samantha said with a grin. Suddenly, her smile weakened a little. "That is, if we can really manage to carry this off."

"Are you kidding? Of course we can!" And then, pulling out one of my very favorite expressions of all time: "It'll be a piece of cake!"

And the truth was that I *was* completely certain that the Bubble Gum Gang was going to pull this little caper off with ease. Especially since I was going to be doing all the hard stuff—and the main thing that was required to do that was the ability to be good at acting.

Betsy's idea really was brilliant. She had come up with the perfect way for three junior high school girls to hang around in a shopping mall, right outside one particular store, for a long time without anyone getting suspicious.

It was beautifully, deliciously simple. Betsy, Samantha and I were going to hold clipboards in our hands and pretend that we were conducting a survey for a school project.

Now, was that inspiration or what?

Once Betsy had come up with the basic idea, it didn't take the sharp minds of the Bubble Gum Gang very long to work out the details. While I had first thought we should pretend we were doing a market-research study—for example, act as if we were work-ing for a clothing company interested in learning more about teenaged girls' attitudes toward certain styles—Samantha wisely pointed out that we were all too young to be hired to do something like that.

That was when Betsy came up with the idea of pretending we were doing a school project. Not only did that make sense, it also gave us an excuse for spending so much time in one place. If one of the mall's security guards came poking around, asking questions, all we had to do was pull out our cover story.

I mean, would any security guard *really* want to stand in the way of three young women striving to achieve academic excellence?

"Okay, here's the plan," I told my two sidekicks once we had bought clipboards at Woolworth's, stashed our schoolbooks in a locker, and taken our places right outside Clothes Circuit. We had just checked inside to make sure Kelly was working. There she was, at the front register. That meant she had a decent view of the area outside of her store—and so we had to stay a few yards away. I was talking in a low voice, wanting to make certain nobody over-heard.

"Kelly is working at the front register again, just like she was on Tuesday when the bracelet incident occurred."

"Check," said Samantha.

"Check," said Betsy.

"We'll have to try really hard to stay out of sight. She has a good view of this part of the mall from where she's standing, so let's make a point of staying a few yards away from the front entrance."

"Check," said Samantha.

"Check," said Betsy. "I know. We can make a point of staying behind those trees they have planted in big pots."

"Or we can stand behind those orange benches," Samantha suggested.

"Check," I said. "Okay. Since I'm the one who's so good at acting, I'll be the one to stop people who are walking by and tell them about this questionnaire we're doing for school."

"Good," Betsy said, looking relieved. "I'd feel kind of funny, just going up to strangers like that."

"I'm not shy about that kind of thing," Samantha added, "but to tell you the truth, I'd be afraid that I'd burst out laughing!"

"Once I find somebody who's willing to answer our survey questions," I went on, "I'll either start asking them the questions myself or else send her over to one of you."

"And in the meantime," Samantha said, "Betsy and I will keep our eyes glued to Clothes Circuit. I'll be in charge of watching the front register, where Kelly is working—"

"And I'll stand over by the pretzel stand so I can get a better view of the register in the back of the store," Betsy volunteered.

"Check," I said once again. This time my voice was kind of a whisper. I was satisfied that our little operation was going to run like clockwork . . . and I was kind of awed by that fact. "Now the girl who's working in the store right now is named Jaimie. She's one of our suspects."

"How do you know for sure that she's Jaimie?" Samantha asked.

"Because when I walked by the store just now, I looked at her name tag."

Samantha nodded. "Good detective work."

"Very slick," Betsy agreed.

"Okay, then, let's do it!"

We took our places. My heart was beating quickly. Was I going to be able to carry this off? I certainly hoped so, since there was an awful lot riding on it. It was time to give it my best shot.

"Excuse me," I said, approaching a girl who looked about sixteen or seventeen. She was walking by Clothes Circuit with a big shopping bag in her hand.

"Yes?" the girl said. Much to my amazement, she had actually stopped walking. She was looking at my clipboard curiously.

"I'm, uh, doing a project for school, and I was wondering if you'd be willing to give me two minutes of your time to help."

"Two minutes?" she repeated. With a little shrug, she said, "Sure, why not?"

"Great!" My first victory! I glanced at the entrance to Clothes Circuit. Nothing much happening in there. Besides, I knew my eagle-eyed associates had the place covered.

"Okay. Here goes," I said, trying my best to sound serious. I looked at my clipboard, where I had quickly jotted down the questions I was going to be asking. "About how much time, on average, would you say you spend doing homework every night?"

"Hmmm." The girl thought for a few seconds. "I guess about an hour. Yes, that sounds right."

"One hour." I was nodding my head as I carefully wrote down, "One hour."

"All right, next question. Do you feel that most teachers give too much homework, too little homework, or just the right amount?"

"Well . . ." The girl was wrapping a strand of her hair around one finger as she pondered that one. Her hesitation gave me a few seconds to sneak another glance over at the store. A shady-looking character was walking by. At least, I thought he was shady-looking. But when he turned around, it turned out it was one of the mall's security guard. He just glanced in my direction and then moved on.

"I'm always complaining about how much homework I have to do," the girl finally replied, "but now that you're asking me, I guess I'd have to admit that most of my teachers give out a fair amount of homework."

I marked the "just about right" box. Much to my amazement, this was actually turning out to be fun.

"Question number three," I said, feeling very important. "Do you ever use a home computer to do your homework?"

"Yes, sometimes."

"And . . . let's see, what grade are you in?"

"I'm a junior at North High School."

"Favorite subject?"

"History."

There. It was done. I looked up at the girl, smiling, ridiculously pleased that my first survey had gone so well.

"That's it! Hey, thanks a lot."

"No problem." The girl walked off, turning back to wave before disappearing into the Shoe Emporium.

Still feeling pleased, I sauntered over to where Samantha was standing.

"I just filled out my first questionnaire," I reported proudly.

"Good for you!" Samantha replied. "Was it hard to do?"

"Not at all!" I was laughing as I added, "Who knows? I might even turn this into a real school project!"

Abruptly I stopped laughing. A sudden movement had caught my eye. My attention turned toward the entrance of Clothes Circuit. A man who could definitely be characterized as a suspicious-looking character was heading inside. "Uh, oh," I breathed. "Check this out."

Samantha turned to look in the same direction. Her mouth fell open as she studied the tall, thin man in the dark raincoat. A raincoat—and there wasn't a cloud in the sky! Now if *that* wasn't fishy, I didn't know what *was*.

"It looks bad," Samantha observed, her eyes still glued to the store.

"What looks bad?" Betsy asked, who had just come over. Her eyes followed our gaze. When she saw what we were looking at, she swallowed hard.

"I was afraid of this," she said in a hoarse voice.

"What?" Samantha and I asked in unison.

"I think it's time for one of us to go in there."

The three of us just looked at each other.

"I'll go," Betsy volunteered. "I have to find out what that man in a trenchcoat is doing, sneaking into Clothes Circuit."

"I don't think he's actually *sneaking*. . . ." Samantha said.

"Betsy is right. Somebody has to investigate. I'll stay here so I can keep going with the survey. Otherwise, somebody might get suspicious."

Sam and I turned to face Betsy. "We'll be backing you up, Betsy. Good luck. And remember: it's all for a good cause!"

We watched as she put her clipboard down on a bench, stood up straight and tall, and walked right in.

"Do you think it's going all right?" I asked, peering into the store, biting my fingernails. By that point, I was simply too nervous to continue with my fake survey.

"I hope so. Look, there's Betsy now. She's pretending to browse," Samantha said. "Look, she's over by that rack of sweaters. Hey, look at that blue one. It's really pretty, and the sign says it's only ten dollars!"

I elbowed her in the side. "Samantha, we're supposed to be sleuthing, not shopping. Look! She's coming out!"

"Done already?" I glanced at my sister, who at the moment was writing up somebody's purchase. As far as I could tell, she hadn't noticed Betsy at all.

"Maybe he threatened her," I whispered. "Or maybe she just couldn't take the heat."

"Sorry, you two." Betsy rolled her eyes upward as she came out of the store. "That suspicious-looking character turned out to be Mr. Deegan, the man who owns the place."

"He's one of our suspects, too," I reminded them.

"Tell you what," said Samantha. "Let's try a new strategy. The old 'divide and conquer.' "

"Divide and conquer?" I repeated. "What's that?"

Betsy fielded that one. "I think what it means, at least in this case, is that I'm in charge of watching Mr. Deegan, Sam is in charge of watching Jaimie, and you're in charge of watching the shoppers."

"Got it." I gave a firm nod of my head. "And thanks for the translation."

It wasn't easy, keeping an eye on the store and acting like a serious student committed to doing a survey. And over the next hour or so, I sometimes got so caught up in learning about how other kids felt about homework that I actually forgot to watch Clothes Circuit at all.

As a matter of fact, I was beginning to lose heart.

The longer we were there, the more likely it seemed that, by the end of the afternoon, we would have learned very little besides the fact that American teenagers are misunderstood when it comes to their opinion on homework and that ten-dollar sweaters sell like hot cakes.

And then, right around the time I was wondering if maybe I should suggest to the other Bubble Gum Gang members that we pack it in for the day, the six-year-old boy bumped into me.

He didn't mean any harm. It's just that, being six years old, he thought it was hilariously funny to let go of his mother's hand and take off, laughing and yelping as he tore across the mall.

"Jeffrey, come back!" his poor mother yelled, breaking into a run herself.

But I didn't notice her at first. And I didn't notice little Jeffrey, either, at least not until he came barreling into me.

"Ooomph!" I yelled as I suddenly found myself stomach to stomach with a quickly moving object. Before I knew what was happening, my clipboard and all my papers went flying. It was a good thing no one else was around, or someone might have ended up with clipboard wounds on his or her body.

Anyway, the next thing I knew, the shrieking Jeffrey was being whisked off by his apologetic mother, who asked me about fifty million times if I was okay. As she led him away, she looked extremely embarrassed about the whole episode. I, meanwhile, was left with the task of retrieving all the papers that had gone flying up into the air, only to come floating down around the mall like snowflakes.

I got most of them right away. But one of them had landed right in front of Clothes Circuit. Right in front of the window, in fact. The very window that was next to the cash register, the one that my sister was using.

And that was how I came to be stooping in front of the store, hidden by the display of a hot pink and orange jogging suit hanging off a wooden mannequin built like a skeleton, with my face not three feet way from my sister. That was how I came to be so close to Kelly that there was absolutely no mistaking what happened.

I watched in amazement as, right in front of me, Kelly looked around nervously and then reached into the display on the counter next to the register, took out a pair of bright papier-mâché earrings, and stuck them underneath the counter, between a couple of pairs of socks neatly stacked there. She looked around again, this time her cheeks beet red. And then, having seen what I saw, which was that nobody in the store had noticed, she went back to straightening up the display of pocketbooks on the shelf behind her.

My head was spinning, but there was one thing I knew: I had to get out of there right away. I picked up that last piece of paper and, still crouching, moved away to the store next door to Clothes Circuit. Then I wove around the benches and trees scattered throughout the walkway of the mall until I got back to my spot in the safety zone.

My head wasn't the only thing that was feeling

weird. I also had sort of a stomachache, the kind I get whenever I'm really upset about something and so I eat an entire box of chocolate cookies, or maybe most of a pint of rocky road ice cream, to make up for it.

All of a sudden, our little sleuthing adventure wasn't fun anymore.

# chapter
## nine

What am I going to *do*? I kept thinking over and over again. I had plopped down on one of the orange benches, trying to get a grip on myself. Never before in my entire life had I felt so confused. I didn't know where to turn, what to do, what to say . . . and I certainly didn't know how I was ever going to face my sister again.

Maybe this is all nothing more than a misunderstanding, I thought. Maybe all Kelly was doing was putting aside a pair of earrings for a particular customer who had been interested in them. . . .

In between a pair of *socks*? another voice inside my head quickly interrupted. Besides, why would she make such a big deal about being secretive if what she was doing was on the level?

My stomach gave a little lurch. Maybe I could get on a bus and go to Omaha, I thought, wishing that, for now, I could crawl into one of those big pots that held the trees I was hiding behind. I have an aunt there that I've never met. Perhaps she'd like to adopt me.

No, that wasn't the answer, I knew. Sooner or later, my parents would find me and make me come back. Besides, I would miss Betsy and Sam. . . .

Betsy and Sam! All of a sudden, there was a bright light shining through the fog. The other members of the Bubble Gum Gang. Surely *they* would know what to do! Somehow, they would find a way to help me through this. After all, wasn't that what our club was all about?

Slowly, I stood up. The moment I had been dreading—the moment it was time to leave my bench— had come. I took a few deep breaths. And then, still clutching my clipboard tightly against my chest, I walked over to where Samantha was standing.

"Hi, Carla," she said brightly. "How's it going?"

"Sam," I replied in a flat voice, "I think it's time for the Bubble Gum Gang to call a conference."

"Need a break?" she asked, looking a little confused.

"What *I* need," I mumbled, "is some good advice."

"Carla, are you okay?" Betsy asked me a few minutes later as the three of us sat at a small table at Burger King. We each had a Coke in front of us, but I had yet to touch mine.

"Oh, I'm fine," I said. "Especially considering the fact that I've recently started giving serious thought to moving to Omaha."

Betsy and Samantha looked at each other.

"Okay, Carla," Betsy said. "What's going on?"

"Did something happen?" Samantha chimed in. "Carla, did you see something inside the store?"

''I guess you could say that.'' I was trying to keep my voice light, but all of a sudden, the full impact of what I had just seen hit me. ''I just saw my sister steal a pair of earrings.''

''You saw *what*?''

''Carla, are you sure?''

I just nodded my head. ''Look, folks, it doesn't take a genius to figure out what's going on here. I saw it with my own eyes. A little boy bumped into me and sent all my papers flying. I had to go right up to the window to pick up one of them. And while I was there, just a few feet away from the cash register, I watched as Kelly took a pair of earrings off the counter, looked around to make sure nobody saw her, and then tucked them under the counter in a pile of socks.''

I sighed, but it was hardly a sigh of relief. Instead, it was a tense, tight sigh. ''I have to conclude that Kelly really did steal the bracelet. Not only that; she's getting ready to steal a pair of earrings, too.''

I took a big sip of my Coke. All of a sudden, I needed to eat. It was as if I was completely empty, and it was such a terrible feeling that I wanted really badly to fill up that hole in the pit of my stomach. ''So what do I do *now*?'' I asked, looking from one of my friends to the other.

Betsy just sat there, staring at the edge of the table. It was Samantha who took charge.

''You have to confront her,'' she said softly.

*''What?''*

With a shrug, she insisted, ''That's the way it has

to be, Carla. Before you do anything, you have to hear her side of the story.''

"Sam is right,'' Betsy said, finally looking at me. "It is possible that all this is a mistake. It could be that what you saw is . . . oh, I don't know. Something other than what it looked like. At any rate, she has the right to explain.''

"Okay,'' I agreed, nodding. "I see your point. But what if it turns out that it's *not* a mistake? What if she really did steal the bracelet—and the earrings—from Clothes Circuit?''

Betsy and Samantha looked at each other.

Wearing this dead serious expression, Betsy said, "You have to tell your parents.''

"My parents!'' I cried. "But . . . but . . .''

"Betsy's right,'' Samantha agreed. "This is serious, Carla. If Kelly really is shoplifting, she could get into a lot of trouble. This is a pretty heavy thing, and it's not your job to deal with that all alone.''

They were right, I knew. I could feel it in the pit of my stomach, down around where a tidal wave of Coke was sloshing around.

I did owe it to Kelly to confront her, to ask her right out what the scene I had just witnessed was all about.

But that didn't mean it was going to be easy.

In fact, as I sat there at Burger King, staring at the straw I had just chewed to pieces, not wanting to look my friends in the eye, I knew that this was going to be one of the most difficult things I had ever done in my life.

* * *

The perfect time to confront Kelly with what I had seen at the mall that afternoon came even sooner than I had expected—certainly sooner than I had hoped. What I had been hoping was that she, too, would suddenly find the idea of moving to Omaha very attractive.

No such luck.

Dinner at the Farrell household went along as usual that evening. Sure, I was a little quiet, but everybody just assumed that was because we were having one of my favorites—macaroni and cheese. Devouring three servings of that, after all, was pretty much guaranteed to keep me occupied.

Then came homework. I was upstairs in my room most of the evening. Kelly, meanwhile, was downstairs on the phone. She was supposed to be setting up a meeting for the yearbook committee, but even from up on the second floor I could hear that there was an awful lot of giggling going on. But I wasn't laughing. Instead, as I plowed through a chapter in my history textbook, I kept watching the clock, dreading the passage of time, knowing that sooner or later, the big hand and the little hand were going to point me in the direction of my sister.

That moment finally arrived. Later that night, right after I had brushed my teeth and put on the oversized T-shirt I usually sleep in, I heard Kelly come upstairs. She went right into her room. I could hear her in there, turning on lights, taking off her shoes, getting ready for bed.

"This is it," I muttered, looking longingly at my own bed. How much easier it would have been to crawl in there, pull the blankets up over my head, and drift off into dreamland!

But the faces of Betsy and Samantha were looming up in front of me, like images on a movie screen. You *have* to do this! they were saying. And I knew they were right.

"Kelly?" I said softly, kind of leaning into her room but still standing in the hall.

She turned around, surprised. "Oh, hi, Carla. I figured you'd be asleep by now."

"Well . . . I kind of have something on my mind." I paused. "Something I'd like to talk to you about."

"Of course!" she said brightly, smiling at me. "What else are big sisters for if not to give wonderful, helpful advice to little sisters?"

"It's, uh, not exactly advice I'm looking for."

"That's okay." Kelly sat down on the edge of her bed, turning her full attention to me. "What's up?"

She looked really pretty. Her eyes were bright, and her cheeks were flushed, probably because she had had a fun evening, talking to her seventeen million friends on the phone. And not only girls, either—if you catch my drift.

For a second there, I was tempted to envy her. But then I remembered why I was here. "Kelly, this is kind of hard for me . . . but here goes. I was, uh, at the mall with my friends today and, uh, I just happened to see you, uh, putting aside a pair of earrings. . . ."

All of a sudden my sister's expression changed. Her smile faded, and the brightness went out of her eyes. All the color drained out of her face.

"You *what*?" she whispered.

"Well, to tell you the truth, it wasn't exactly an *accident* that I saw what happened with those earrings. You see, Samantha and Betsy and I decided that we'd try to find out who really had stolen the bracelet from Mr. Deegan's store. . . ."

Kelly was staring at me with pure rage in her eyes. "How *dare* you sneak around, watching me while I'm at work!" she screamed. "What are you, a spy or something? Of all the sneaky, low-down things to do. . . . And to think that I *trusted* you! Here I thought you were somebody who really cared about me!"

"I wasn't sneaking around! And I wasn't spying on you! All I was doing was trying to find out who was shoplifting at Clothes Circuit! I only wanted to help."

"Help!" she yelled back at me. *"Help!"*

"Kelly, listen to me. We have to talk about this," I pleaded. "I want to know what really happened. I want to hear your side of it!"

"My side of *what*?" she shot back. "You're the one who's the spy! You're the one who can't be trusted!"

"Kelly, please! I just want to . . . Can't we calm down and talk about this?"

And then, instead of shrieking at me some more or throwing things or stomping out of the room—all things I was totally prepared for—Kelly did something I never would have expected. She burst into tears.

Without stopping to wonder whether or not it was

the right thing to do, I went over to the bed, dropped down beside her, and put my arms around her.

"Look," I said gently, "I have an idea. I was so stuffed with macaroni and cheese that I skipped dessert tonight, and I know for a fact there's still half a chocolate cake left in the refrigerator. How about if you and I go downstairs to the kitchen and have some? With a big glass of ice-cold milk. What do you think? I know I could use a snack."

Kelly just nodded. Her pretty face was still streaked with tears as I led her down to the kitchen.

Fortunately, Mom and Dad were in the den, glued to the TV, absorbed in some documentary. Kelly and I had the kitchen to ourselves. Once we were in there, I kept busy, glad to have a distraction for at least a few minutes. I needed time to try to sort things out, to vacuum the fuzz out of my mind and start thinking clearly. In the meantime I filled two glasses with milk. Then I put the left-over chocolate cake on the kitchen table. I cut myself a big hunk and left the knife on the plate so Kelly could help herself. Just as I expected, she totally ignored it.

Finally, I couldn't wait any longer. Kelly and I were sitting face-to-face at the table. I was armed with my cake and my milk, my fork already in my hand, ready for anything.

"Okay. So what's going on?" I asked in a soft voice. The last thing I wanted to do was sound accusing. "Or is there some reasonable explanation why you hid that pair of papier-mâché earrings under the counter this afternoon?"

Kelly's shoulders were slumped low. She couldn't even look me in the eye.

"The only explanation is the obvious one," she said dully. "I was getting ready to take them. Before I left work today, I got them out from under the counter when nobody was looking and put them in my purse." She took a deep breath. "I'm the one who took the bracelet, too."

"Why did you do it?" I stuffed a big chunk of cake into my mouth. Even before I had swallowed it, I was balancing another piece on my fork.

Kelly shrugged. Her eyes were still fixed on the table as she said, "It was such beautiful jewelry. I didn't have the money to buy it, but I still wanted it."

"But didn't you think about the fact that what you were doing was shoplifting?"

She nodded. "I know. But I wanted that bracelet and the earrings so much. And it seemed so unfair that I really, really wanted them and I didn't have enough money to buy them. I kept thinking that it would be weeks before I got my first paycheck, that they could even have been sold out by then. . . ." Her voice trailed off.

"But, Kelly, I just don't get it!" I cried. "You have so much going for you! You're pretty, you're smart, you're popular . . . and here you had landed yourself your dream job. And yet you stole! You took such a crazy risk! And you almost got caught. But even so, you went back and did it a second time!"

I paused for a few seconds, just staring at her.

"Kelly, why on earth would you do something to

screw it all up? Why do something that, in the end, is only going to hurt *you*?''

''Well . . . well . . .'' Kelly sputtered. She never did come up with an answer. Instead, she turned to me and said, ''Well, Carla, what about *you*?''

I was so startled that I put down the forkful of chocolate cake. ''What are you talking about?''

She took a deep breath. ''The way you eat, Carla.''

''*What?*'' I had been caught totally off guard.

''I never said anything before because I didn't want to hurt your feelings. But . . . but the way you're always sneaking food, eating everything you can get your hands on, all the while acting as if you're fooling Mom and Dad, outsmarting them or something. . . .''

''I don't do that!''

''Oh, no? Then what about this summer? What about that camp you went to?''

I was in a mild state of shock. Here we were supposed to be talking about Kelly, and all of a sudden we were instead talking about me.

''Camp Breezy Pines? What about it?''

''What *about* it? Carla, you were there for eight whole weeks, but you hardly lost any weight at all.''

''Kelly, I can't help it if I happen to be one of those people who puts on weight more easily than everybody else.''

''Did you really think that sneaking in cookies from fancy mail order companies was going to help?''

''How did you know about that?'' I demanded. As

far as I had known, that little secret had remained between my parents and me.

"I do have ears, you know."

"Well, it only happened twice. Three times, maybe . . ." I could feel my face turning beet red. I was wishing that big chunk of chocolate cake would suddenly just disappear.

"Here Mom and Dad were spending all this money to send you to Camp Breezy Pines to help you lose weight—and you did everything you could to screw it up. It was your big chance to get thin, and you blew it, Carla. On *purpose*. Talk about someone getting in her own way!

"And as if that weren't bad enough, it's as if now you're trying your hardest to gain *back* the weight you did lose! And you have, haven't you? You've started putting on weight again, even though you were supposed to be spending the summer learning how not to."

Suddenly, as if I were coming out of a fog, I could see past the anger, past the feeling of being attacked, past feeling like doing anything and everything I could to defend myself. And what I saw was that Kelly was right.

And that I had been wrong. *Dead* wrong.

Just like Kelly, I was somebody who had everything going for me. I had good friends and a great family. I did well in school. I had a special talent, acting. I was even kind of pretty, or I would be if my face were a little thinner.

And what was I doing? Getting in my own way.

Ruining it for myself. Making myself miserable, over something that only I could control.

I was hurting myself. And *only* myself.

I never thought I'd live to see the day, but all of a sudden that big piece of fresh chocolate cake sitting in front of me looked totally unappetizing. In fact, I don't think I could have eaten it if somebody offered me a zillion dollars.

"Kelly," I said in a soft voice, "you're right."

"What?" Now it was my sister's turn to be startled. "What did you say?"

"I said that you're right. That *is* what I've been doing. Eating all the time. Using food as a way to help me feel good when I was feeling bad—or even using it to make me feel even better when I was already feeling okay. Stuffing my face every chance I got, even sneaking around as if I were being really clever. And all along I've only been hurting myself."

There were tears in my eyes as I said, "And from now on, I'm going to try really hard to stop doing it."

I blinked a few times. As much as part of me wanted to cry, part of me felt like shrieking with joy. It was as if I had discovered some wonderful secret. Yes, I hated being fat. I hated having kids make fun of me. I hated being self-conscious about walking across the front of a room. I hated not being able to wear the cool clothes I was always seeing in stores. Most of all, I hated seeing a part in a play that I deserved, the part of Emily Webb, go to someone who couldn't act her way out of a paper bag.

And finally I understood that if all that was ever going to change, I was going to have to be the one to make it happen.

"Hey, Kelly?" I suddenly said.

"Yes, Carla?"

"Thanks. Thanks a lot."

I got up from the kitchen table and gave my sister a hug. I wasn't quite sure how she'd react. But she gave me a big hug right back. And then she smiled at me, this nervous, almost scared kind of smile.

"Carla, will you do me a favor?"

"Sure," I replied, grinning. "I owe you one."

"Will you come with me while I talk to Mom and Dad? I think it's about time they found out what's been going on."

"Kelly, I'd be honored." Then, looking over at her and smiling, I added, "After all, what are sisters for?"

# chapter
## ten

"All right, everybody," cried Ms. Hart, taking her place at the front of the auditorium, clutching her copy of the script. "I know it's the end of the week and you're all eager to get home, but you know that old saying, 'The show must go on.' "

I don't know about the rest of the drama club, but I, for one, couldn't have cared less that it was Friday afternoon. It didn't bother me at all that, except for the group of us gathered together in the auditorium, the school building was totally deserted. It was time for the first run-through of Act Two, and all I cared about was getting up there on stage.

And this time, I really *was* going to be the best darned Mrs. Webb anyone had ever seen.

"Okay. All the characters who appear in Act Two, take your places!" called Ms. Hart.

Thanks to my talk with Kelly the night before—and the better understanding of myself that had come out of it—my enthusiasm for show biz had returned. So what if Wendy Lipton couldn't act? So what if I hadn't gotten the exact part I wanted? That didn't mean the world had come to an end. That didn't mean I couldn't enjoy being a part of *Our Town*.

And that didn't mean that, one day, I wouldn't be able to get the parts I wanted. Not if I was willing to work for them.

"Hey, Carla, got a second?" Andrew Morris was suddenly next to me, having made a beeline in my direction as I headed up the aisle toward the stage with a bunch of the other kids.

"Sure. What's up?"

I must admit, I was kind of surprised. I hardly even knew Andrew. In fact, the only two things I knew about him were that he was a terrific actor and that the role of Stage Manager seemed custom-made for him.

He spoke to me in a low voice. "I don't know if you've noticed, but this production has got a real problem on its hands." With his chin, he gestured in Wendy Lipton's direction. "Our Emily is hardly on her way to Broadway. If the drama club is going to do the terrific job I'm hoping we'll do, somebody had better take that girl aside and give her a few pointers."

I hesitated. "What are you suggesting?"

"Well . . . look at it this way. You're obviously better than any of us when it comes to acting. And, uh, I guess I could consider myself a fairly close second. I mean, I've always been told I have kind of a knack for it, too." Andrew was turning a rather interesting shade of pink. "Anyway, I thought maybe you and I could get together with old Wendy some time next week and, you know, help her out a little."

He looked over at her once again, this time letting out a loud sigh. "She certainly could use it."

I laughed. "And here I thought I was the only one who had noticed."

"Are you kidding? My four-year-old brother would have noticed!"

Suddenly his face grew serious. "By the way, Carla, I've been meaning to tell you that I thought your reading at the audition was incredible. It totally blew me away. You've got real talent."

Andrew wasn't the only one who was capable of turning the color of a rose garden.

"Well, *thank* you. That really means a lot, coming from you," I said. I just hoped I sounded as sincere as I felt.

"Anyway, what do you say? Do you agree that we owe it to the Drama Club to teach Wendy a few basic lessons in the art of performing on the stage?"

"Definitely. We also owe it to Thornton Wilder, who wrote the play in the first place!"

"All right, everybody, let's get started," called Ms. Hart. "Where is my Stage Manager? And Mrs. Webb? Where is my Mrs. Webb?"

I held my hand up high in the air and waved. I was wearing a great big grin as I called back, "Your Mrs. Webb is over here!"


"So what'll it be?" I asked on Friday evening, sticking my head into the refrigerator and poking around. "There's still a piece of chocolate cake left. There's root beer—Betsy, I know how much you like root beer. And Sam, there's milk, if you want some."

"Anything is fine," Betsy insisted with a wave of her hand.

"We'll have whatever you're having," Samantha added.

I turned around and chuckled. "What *I'm* having is an apple. Last night I made a pact with myself. From now on, I'm going to change the way I eat. It's time to undo some of my old habits."

I took a long hard look at that last piece of chocolate cake. Want to know the truth? For all the appeal it had, it could have been lump of clay. I knew there would be other pieces of cake in my life . . . but not right now. For now, what mattered to me most was changing a situation that had been making me miserable for a long time—a situation that I had never before taken the slightest bit of responsibility for. And bypassing that cake and instead reaching for the fruit bowl was the very first step.

"An apple sounds good to me," Betsy said. "Sam?"

"Count me in."

"I guess last night turned out to be pretty important for you," Betsy commented once I had joined them at the kitchen table. The three of us were munching away noisily.

"Yes, I guess it was," I agreed. "Who would have ever thought such an awful thing could turn out so well? And coming to understand myself a whole lot better was only part of it. I think I now understand my sister better than I ever did before, too.''

I hesitated for a moment, replaying scenes from that afternoon, as well as the evening before, in my mind. Sure, it had been tough, confronting Kelly. But that turned out to be nothing compared to sitting down with my parents for a long, hard talk. My stomach was playing hopscotch as I watched Kelly tell my parents about what had happened.

And, just as I had expected, they went through a whole string of emotions. First they were confused. Then they were unable to believe what Kelly was telling them. Next came a furious stage, during which she got grounded for a month. Fortunately, that one didn't last too long. Soon they moved on to trying to get to the bottom of what was going on with my sister.

But even those two scenes turned out to be easier than the last. That afternoon, right after school, I had gone to Clothes Circuit with Kelly so she could tell Mr. Deegan everything. Naturally, she returned both the bracelet and the earrings. I wasn't surprised that Mr. Deegan fired her on the spot. It was what both Kelly and I had been expecting. And I wasn't surprised by the long lecture he gave her on what a bad thing she had done. But I was surprised when, just before we left, he told her that she had done a brave thing, coming forth with the truth.

I had to agree. Even though Kelly was in tears by then, even though she had managed to screw up her dream job at Clothes Circuit, even though she felt so bad that all she could say, over and over again, was that she'd never do anything like that again . . . I was still pretty proud of her for having the guts to take responsibility for what she had done.

Almost as if she were a mind reader, Betsy said, "I guess that nobody's life is ever as perfect as you may think it is."

"Even people who look as if everything comes to them easily," Samantha added.

We were all silent for a few seconds, thinking about that. It certainly had turned out to be true in Kelly's case. I felt a little sheepish about the way I had always treated her, acting as if she didn't have a problem or a care in the world. But I had learned a real lesson. And now that she had come down off that pedestal I had put her up on, I had a feeling that we were going to end up being pretty good friends.

Of course, we still had a way to go. . . .

"Hey, are you two almost done with your apples?" Betsy suddenly said.

I looked down at mine and saw that I had already gobbled up almost all of mine.

"I'm done." I couldn't resist adding, "Why, is it time for dessert?"

"You bet!" There was a twinkle in Betsy's green eyes as she reached into her pocket and brought out three pieces of bubble gum. "Here, I think we deserve these. After all, we might not be the best sleuths in the world, but we *did* manage to get to the bottom of this mystery!"

Laughing, I reached for a piece of gum and began to unwrap it. Meanwhile, Betsy and Sam were doing the exact same thing. And then, completely in uni-son, we all popped them into our mouths.

"How sweet it is!" I cried.

And the taste of the bubble gum was only a small part of it.

# About the Author

Cynthia Blair grew up on Long Island, earned her B.A. from Bryn Mawr College in Pennsylvania, and went on to get an M.S. in marketing from M.I.T. She worked as a marketing manager for food companies but has abandoned the corporate life in order to write. She lives on Long Island with her husband and her son.